T0095463

IN AND AROUND
THE CARIBBEAN

Stories, People and Places

Other books by Henry Toledano

The Bitter Seed
A Sort of Justice
The Modern Library Price Guide
Goreyography
Nasty Stories and a Fable with a Happy Ending

IN AND AROUND THE CARIBBEAN

Stories, People and Places

By Henry Toledano

iUniverse, Inc.
Bloomington

IN AND AROUND THE CARIBBEAN
Stories, People and Places

iUniverse books may be ordered through booksellers or by contacting:

iUniverse
1663 Liberty Drive
Bloomington, IN 47403
www.iuniverse.com
1-800-Authors (1-800-288-4677)

ISBN: 978-1-4697-3253-4 (sc)
ISBN: 978-1-4697-3254-1 (ebk)

Printed in the United States of America

iUniverse rev. date: 02/14/2012

CONTENTS

STORIES

Flight 407   9

Mr Davidson 's Secret   15

Pearl   41

The Colonial Secretary`   71

The Mother-in-law   91

TRAVEL

Nassau: No Thank You   121

St Thomas   131

Mario and His Pergola   135

Martinique   145

Anything Can Happen in Trinidad   149

Ms Stollmeyer's Guest House   153

Trinidad to Brazil   161

MORE STORIES

The Editor   179

The Witch   189

Reading Palms   209

AUTHOR'S NOTE

I traveled round the world in 1960/61 and the travel articles were the result of my trip through the Caribbean. The short stories were written between 1960 and 1970 and both articles and stories have been revised, though basically not changed. The short stories are entirely fictional and any resemblance of names and characters of actual people, dead or alive, is purely coincidental.

Flight 407

It was dull and windy and I anticipated the worst. I have tried tablet after tablet, pill after pill on this or that person's recommendation, but none of them seem to do me any good. I have always been a nervous traveler, and notwithstanding that old adage which says one gets used to things, expect I always will be.

The trip started in London. I flew to Luxemburg and took Air International to The Bahamas. The flight was cheap, that's why I opted for it, though I knew nothing of the airline. This made me nervous, though I was somewhat reassured when I saw that the plane was a Super Constellation, an aircraft I had flown on many times

My seat was away from the window. I am a fussy traveler: everything has to be just so; my seat has to be over the wings because it gives me an added feeling of security; the seat angle must be just right otherwise I get a headache; I like to be near the window because I have control of the ventilation. I always find planes very stuffy, and if the air is not full on me feel as sick as a dog.

While airborne, I sit back quietly and relax, or rather try and relax; but sometimes if the weather is unusually fine I do not mind reading a light novel. I never eat when in a plane and do my best to discourage conversation with my neighbor.

Not only was I jittery flying Air International, but I was not over the wings, was away from the window and the weather was ominous. I prepared myself for an unpleasant journey.

My traveling companion was a certain Mr. Milio. I was ready to dislike him even before meeting him. No sooner had I got myself comfortable than he wanted to get through to his seat. He was a big man, tall with hefty features. He reminded me of a pregnant cow. I took him for an American. His face was red, big to match his body, with a loud jovial air about it and it seemed as though he had every intention of enjoying the journey. I had just got myself comfortable

9

again when I felt a prod on my right elbow.

"I'm Milio. I hear you're English too."

I gaped.

"You're not English?" I asked somewhat tactlessly.

"You bet I am. You don't think I look American do you? English to the backbone, that's me." And just to prove it he pulled out his passport.

I said I hadn't given his nationality a thought.

"I say old boy, you've forgotten to fasten your seat belt."

I gave him an icy look, then politely thanked him. He had the perfect Oxford accent, which only those who have never been to the university have, and his cliches were those of a Public School man who had never quite grown up. I surmised he was one of those Englishmen who traveled about the globe without ever setting foot in England. He must have been in his late thirties. The engines roared, the plane surged forward and a few moments later we were airborne.

"I say old man you can loosen your seat belt now." I felt a prod on my elbow.

"Thanks.

I did not like Milio. We were still climbing. Thick grey clouds streamed past the portholes like some threatening monster and I felt a nervous pang run through my stomach. I was beginning to feel sick.

"Have a cigar old chap --- Havana special. I can recommend it"

"No thanks," I replied, more conscious of the portentous clouds than anything else.

"Hope you don't mind if I do." And he proceeded to light one.

I threw him an angry glance. I have never understood why people want to smoke at all. (I have always endorsed that very admirable definition of a cigarette --- 'fire at one end and a fool at the other'.) But cigars are just about the last straw. They have all the disadvantages of a cigarette in addition to a few more of their own. They are ridiculously expensive, hideous to look at and their smell is nauseating to those who do not smoke them. I have never held Sir Walter Raleigh in high esteem (he introduced cigars into England) and have always considered the damage he did the British public far outstripped the good he may have done in other fields[1].

We were now moving up above the clouds and I was relieved to catch an occasional glimpse of blue sky. The air hostess brought us a selection of magazines, but I did not take one and was disappointed to see that Milio refused one also.

"I always say it's such a shame reading when you can talk. Don't you think?"

"I personally enjoy reading," I replied rather coldly.

He then said he had just the thing for me and fished out from his pocket a Modern Library book of collected short stories.

"You'll enjoy these. I recommend *The Letter*. It's really very good, but if you like Hemingway you can always read *The Snows of Kilimanjaro*. But of course I've climbed the mountain and it rather knocks the bottom out of the story. Then there's a story by Lawrence. Ah yes, here it is."

I thanked him and said I did not feel like reading at the present moment.

Much to my horror he started telling me about *The Prussian Officer*. I have always hated being told a story at second hand, but when it is told me in a plane that is the end. I closed my eyes and tried to sleep, but Milio's monotonous drawl went on and on, and I had the feeling that Lawrence's story was as long as a Russian novel. All the while he leisurely exhaled his nauseating tobacco smoke.

"What do you think of it?" he finished up.

"Very good. I'll have to read it," I replied not having listened to a word of it and fully resolved never to read another book by Lawrence for as long as I lived.

---

[1] Columbus introduced tobacco into Europe, but it was Sir Walter Raleigh who first brought it to England.

Milio then got on to what I gathered was his pet subject. He started talking about himself. I listened. I have always found people so much more interesting when they talk about themselves. So many people talk about matters they know little about, so it is quite a pleasure to listen to those who talk on a subject with which they are well acquainted.

Milio had gone to Egypt shortly after the war and he liked the Middle East so much that he never returned to England. He had gone into business first with an English firm and then an American one. He had traveled up and down Africa, the Far East and knew the Near East like the lines on his hand.

Business now necessitated for him to go to Nassau, then he was off to South America. I gathered he was some kind of semi-precious stones merchant. He was single because he liked his independence. He talked about my friend John, or my pal Peter, Al, Donald etc, when he spoke of this or that celebrity, and I was led to understand that who he didn't know wasn't worth knowing.

It seemed as though he had money for he met his old pal so and so at the Semiramis in Cairo, and another at the King David in Jerusalem, or business had taken him to Istanbul and he had stayed at the Hilton. Of course in Nassau he would be staying at the Nassau Beach, five miles out of town, but that didn't matter as he would hire a car. He was surprised to learn I would have to rent a room in a private home. Apparently In Rio he would be staying at the Copacabana.

I think he guessed what I was thinking, for he then started telling me that he had a first class ticked, but there had been a mixup and as he had to be in Nassau the next day he took whatever he could get.

He called the air hostess and in French, which I spoke, asked her how much Air International paid her; when she told him he said she could get three times as much working in a hotel in Bayreuth.

At about twelve thirty he gave me a prod and asked me whether I wanted a drink. We had moved into some portentous clouds and it was quite bumpy. I was feeling a bit under the weather, and felt sure I must have looked green. The mention of a drink made me lunge for my bag.

"You're not feeling sick are you old man?"

I wasn't in a position to answer his ridiculous question and he rang for the hostess and ordered himself a whisky.

"Do you know this one?" He went straight on: "Goha had lost five piasters down the drain. So he calls a beggar and promises him five piasters to recover the coin. Ha. Ha. Good isn't it?" He rocked and rolled with laughter.

As best I could I smiled politely.

That set him off: more Goha stories from Egypt, then Jewish jokes, Chinese jokes, a few semi-dirty ones. I don't know what he didn't try to keep me amused. I found him very tedious and it was most exhausting to laugh at what I thought wasn't in the least bit funny. Sometimes if I didn't smile he would explain the joke so that in the end I found it required less effort to laugh at everything he said than to endure his explanations of the obvious.

After each joke he laughed. I got the impression he thought himself quite a wit.

The hostess, now donned as waitress, served him lunch.

"Aren't you going to eat anything old man? It'll do you the world of good. There's nothing like having something to do; it takes your mind off yourself."

I said I wasn't hungry. He plunged into his food with relish and I thought he would give me a few moments quiet, but I was wrong for it seemed that he was fully resolved to keep me entertained. He hadn't told me all his stories yet.

I could stand it no longer so I politely excused myself. There were just over three hours to go before we were due in Nassau, and I decided that, if possible, I would change my seat. I told the hostess of my desire, and she arranged the thing for me. An American gentleman at the back of the plane very kindly volunteered his seat and I was pleased to relax next to a benign old lady who I felt sure would not disturb me. I was glad to have escaped Milio.

The rest of the journey passed quickly. Most of the time I was in a semi-doze and it wasn't until the steward drew my attention to the fasten seat belt sign that I realized we had almost arrived.

On the way out of the plane and on the tarmac towards the terminal I hurried to catch up with gentleman who had given me his seat. He was an average sized man, young, dressed in sports jacket and grey flannels. He was walking briskly. I caught up with him.

"It was very good of you to give me your seat," I said.

"You're welcome," he smiled.

I then thanked him more effusively.

"You're welcome, You're welcome," he repeated in a somewhat business-like manner. There was a pause and he went on more chirpily: "I don't blame you wanting to move. Rather a dull fellow this Milio. I couldn't get a word out of him. Not a word. Unsociable fellow."

I smiled politely and we went into the terminal.

Mr Davidson's Secret

It was ten to four and Mrs Davidson's appointment was not until 4:00. Dr Fleury closed his eyes and leaning back in his chair let his mind wander. This was his first moment of peace all day. It had been an exceptionally busy morning at the hospital and in the afternoon, instead of having his accustomed siesta, he had had to go to court to give evidence. The case had not been particularly important and he was not long in the witness stand, but nevertheless he had to wait around and that had tired him. Dr Fleury was not a young man; his health was poor and it exhausted him not to rest in the afternoon. He would have liked to cancel Mrs Davidson, but it was too late now, and it was against his principles to send somebody away once the appointment was made. He breathed deeply as he relaxed. He made no attempt to control the stream of his thoughts. He hoped that Mrs Davidson would not come and he resolved to tell his secretary to send her away if she came after 4:15.

Dr Fleury was a small man. His face was long, his cheeks puffy with drooping layers of skin under the eyes. His lips curled upwards and gave him a sensual air. He wore a white shirt, dark blue sweater, light grey flannels. Everything about him was neat and precise. On the left hand of his index finger he wore a heavy gold ring. If a stranger in town had passed him in the street he would not have noticed him. Notwithstanding his nondescript appearance most people in Nassau would have recognized him. He was a leading ex-Harley street psycho-analyst.

He had come to The Bahamas five years earlier. It had always been his ambition to spend his declining years in the sun, so that when his doctor told him he must leave England and move to a warmer climate it had been no hardship for him to make the move. He had chosen Nassau for several reasons. In the first place he had a sentimental affection for the place, for he had met his wife there and he had fond memories of his marriage. Secondly, there would be no difficulty in transferring funds from England to the colony as it was within the Commonwealth. The doctor intended to live in the utmost comfort. Thirdly, and this reason had weighed strongly in his mind, he had no intention of retiring completely. Nassau was only a thirty minute flight to Miami and this would enable him, he thought, to attract patients from the mainland. His reputation, he imagined, would provide him with more patients than he needed and thus enable him to be choosy in whom he saw.

Dr Fleury's day was perfectly regular. He rose at 8:15, had breakfast and quickly scanned the few odd pages of the Nassau Guardian. He then showered and got dressed and by 9:30 was ready to go to the hospital. He was not on the hospital staff, but acted as a consultant, for which he took no pay. Life had been good to him and he felt it only right that he should return some of the blessings he had received by helping those less fortunate. At about noon he left the hospital and went to the Carlton or Ambassador's for a drink. Lunch and his siesta followed. At 3:30 he was ready to see his private patients. These he saw on the ground floor of his house. The day ended with a light meal and a couple of hours bridge.

The room where Fleury saw his patients was medium sized, gently air-conditioned and immaculate. The blinds were drawn, but the room was still fairly bright for it faced east and the sun penetrated the individual slats of the shades. Besides a large desk there was an easy chair, a couch and against two of the walls light brown bookcases filled with scholarly tomes. The atmosphere was friendly and aimed to put patients at their ease. Dr Fleury did not believe in any one psychological theory to the exclusion of others. His approach was eclectic: every person was different and had to be treated accordingly. However, with first time patients the reception was always Adlerian[1]. The blinds were slightly open so that the room was bright. The patient was offered the

---

[1]

Positive, bright with an air of optimism

comfort of the arm chair.

As Dr Fleury sat idly in his chair his mind wandered to the Davidsons. He recalled having met them at one or two cocktail parties. He remembered that Mrs Davidson was an attractive woman, tall and slender with a fine figure and aristocratic bearing. Mr Davidson was also, he recalled, a handsome man, also slim, a little taller than his wife, but about him there was something awkward. If his memory served him well Davidson spoke slowly, deliberately, stressing facts as though he had to avoid expressing an opinion. Of course the doctor realized this was only a first impression and it could be wrong or he could be mixing him up with somebody else. He adjusted the decorative ink well on his desk. He wondered what Mrs Davidson wanted to see him about. His experience had taught him that a wife often came to see him on her husband's behalf. Rarely was it the other way about. Was Mr or Mrs going to be his patient, he wondered? While he was thus contemplating his secretary came into the room and announced that Mrs Davidson had arrived.

"Show her in please."

The young lady withdrew and a moment later ushered in Mrs Davidson. The doctor rose and shook hands with her. He indicated the arm chair with a sweep of his hand and then seated himself behind the desk again. After a pause he asked why she had come.

Mrs Davidson, who was sitting very upright in her light blue dress, very open at the neck, spoke as though she had given very careful thought to what she was going to say: "I've come about my husband," she began and went on immediately without embarrassment. "I would like you to see him if you would. Of course, he doesn't know I'm here and if he did he would be furious. I've tried to persuade him to see you of his own accord, but he won't. I think once he knows I've talked to you it'll be easier for him to come. That's what I'm hoping anyway."

She then chatted on for a few minutes, saying that she knew all about the doctor from when she lived in England, how she had been influenced by his books and what a singular opportunity it was to find him living in Nassau. She did so hope that he would see her husband.

"What exactly is the problem Mrs Davidson?"

"Drink," she replied crisply and then repeated herself. "Quite simply drink". She paused and then went on: "It's got steadily worse ever since we've been here. At first I didn't attach much importance to it. I didn't like it, of course. But then everybody else here seemed to drink more than to in England. Dick talked a lot about settling in. We hadn't been married very long and I didn't want to nag. I thought that with time Dick would realize he was drinking more than what was good for him." She shrugged. "I was wrong. Dick began to drink more and more. Soon I realized he couldn't do without it. I begged him to stop or, anyway, drink less. It was ruining his life, I told him, and mine. And it wasn't good for his health and his job would be affected. He liked his work. Nothing did any good. He promised to drink less and for a few days he would keep his word. Then he'd begin all over again. A little while ago I persuaded him to have a check-up. He was examined from head to toe. The doctor said he had a constitution of iron—he was in fine physical shape___ nothing wrong with him. I then tried to get him to see you, but he laughed and said he'd just been to one doctor and couldn't see any point going to another.

"All this was just about six months ago. I didn't see what my next step was going to be. It all looked hopeless. Every day Dick seemed to get a little worse. Now and again he took a day off and I would ring his boss and say he was ill. Of course, Lawson, that's Dick's boss, knew everything; but he'd always be very sympathetic and hoped that Dick would soon be better. Lawson has no qualifications and if this wasn't Nassau wouldn't be where he is. He's only too pleased to have a first class engineer like Dick under him. Dick, with his know how, keeps the plant going and Lawson gets the praise and in return is tight lipped about Dick's drinking. If I'd known the job was going to be as it is I would never have accepted to come out here in the first place. But Dick said it was a good job and that the pay was excellent, not that that particularly mattered in view of our circumstances. Though I did think that if he had a well paying job he would develop more self respect, for I felt he was already beginning to go downhill in England. I was wrong about that too. The job is something of a sinecure. Dick tells me there isn't much to do and if he takes a day off now and again it doesn't much matter.

"Dick's a good engineer. His qualifications are first rate and in time he could go places. We would have done better to stay in England, but he insisted that a few years abroad would help him in his career. What I didn't realize, but do now, is that the magnet was not a job, but drink. Here everybody drinks. Liquor is cheap. He's far from the interference and criticism of family and friends. Dick is still young and there's time for him to pull himself together. Here he's in a rut and I can only see him getting into a deeper one. His contract expires in nine months and I had hoped that we would return to England. However, recently things came to a head. Dick has made it quite clear that he wants to sign up for another three years. We've had fearful rows about it. I begged him to change his mind. I've pointed out the harm he was doing himself. And me. There was no future for him in The Bahamas, I told him. I wanted kids and this wasn't a place to bring them up. He wouldn't listen to anything I said. He was adamant. He didn't like England. He liked Nassau and intended to stay. That was final. When I realized he meant what he said I plucked up courage and decided to see you." She stopped abruptly and then said quite simply: "Can you help?

"I can't make any promises," replied the doctor, "but I'll do my best. ."

Mrs Davidson was effusive: "I'm so grateful to you Doctor. I can't thank you enough. You don't know how much better you make me feel already. If only you could get Dick to leave this dreadful place that would be half the battle I'm sure."

Fleury was inclined to contradict her; to tell her there was nothing wrong with Nassau; the problem was her husband's; there were other reasons for his drinking. He restrained himself and said: "I wonder if I could ask you a few questions?".

"Certainly."

The doctor confined himself to facts. "How long have you been married?"

"A little under four years."

"How long did you know your husband before you married?"

"About six months."

"Were you both in love at the time?"

"Yes."

"Did your parents approve of the match?"

"Yes."

"Did your husband's?"

"Yes."

"Have you any children?"

"No."

"You said you wanted to have children?"

"Yes, but Dick is in no hurry. He says there's plenty of time."

Fleury was making notes on a large pad. He continued: "What is your faith?" "Catholic."

"What about your husband?"

"He's Catholic too. He converted about a year before we married."

'Why did he do that, do you know?"

"He said that he wanted to: he believed."

"What was your reaction and that of his family?"

"Everybody was delighted. I'm Catholic and my uncle is a Bishop."

"Have either you or you husband been to a priest about your predicament?"

"I have, but since Dick has taken to drink he won't go near a priest. He hasn't been to confession now for nearly two years."

"What did the priest say?"

"He told me to pray."

The doctor looked at his watch. It was nearly 5:00. "I'm afraid Mrs Davidson your time is up. If you can persuade your husband to come and see me I'll do my best to help. I suggest you make an appointment for him with my secretary. You can always cancel if he absolutely refuses to come."

He stood up and accompanied her to the door.

The following week on the Thursday, punctually on the dot of 6:00 Fleury's secretary ushered in Mr Davidson. He was, as he remembered him, tall and slender with a long face, dark eyes and a mop of long black hair. It was a face of contradictions, thought the doctor. There was determination in the eyes and creases around the mouth which gave the impression of self discipline. The chin, however, was weak and the lips were somewhat thick and sensual as though hungry for something. Davidson's overall bearing was a mixture of defiance and awkwardness as he stood facing the analyst.

"Won't you sit down," invited the doctor.

Gingerly the young man seated himself and stared at Fleury.

"Your wife has already told me the reason for your visit."

Davidson stopped him from going on. "I'll have you know doctor that this wasn't my idea. I don't believe in this psychology business. I've come to please my wife. I'll give you six months, then if there's no change I quit. I'll do my best to cooperate, because I can't see any point in paying your exorbitant fees if I don't. OK, what now?"

Fleury showed no sign that his patient's threatening manner had phased him. His face was calm and when he spoke his voice was even. "Perhaps it would be a good idea if you answered a few questions to start with so that I can get to know something about you?"

The doctor then proceeded to ask the usual questions of new patients.

Briefly the information he extracted in that first hour was as follows:

- Davidson was 29. He was born in London and was the eldest child of three. His father was in the House of Lords and, being the eldest son, he would succeed him. Davidson had been to Harrow and Cambridge. Subsequently he had got a commission in the army and done much of his military service in West Africa. He had not been particularly good at games, but had acquired a good second class degree in his Mechanical Tripos. His parents were in good health and there was no record of excessive drinking in the family. His father, Lord K------ spoke frequently in the House of Lords and was well known for his high moral tone on such issues as family values, gambling, prostitution, alcoholism and the like. (Fleury sensed his patient had perhaps rebelled against his principled father.) Davidson had become a Catholic soon after he was discharged from the army. His explanation wasn't too clear to the doctor, but the gist was that he liked the precepts of Catholicism, its rituals, its inflexible moral code, the unswerving views of right and wrong. Other Christian denominations, he said, seemed to offer no anchor: edicts changed with the times—there was nothing you could hold on to. He didn't like that. "Truth is an absolute." he postulated. Immediately after conversion he frequently went to confession. He drank a little. He had acquired the taste in the army. He was forgiven his sins, but all the while continued to drink, though moderately. He met his wife within a year of being back in London. The fact that her family was staunchly Catholic appealed to him. He loved her of course. His newfound faith, he thought, would be strengthened with marriage and he had little doubt, at the time, that his drinking would subside. It was not be. He struggled with himself. He tried various therapies—detox clinics, Alcoholics Anonymous, counseling. Nothing worked for long. It was then that he hit on the idea to go abroad, away from the oppressive atmosphere of his father and in-laws. He knew he was hurting his wife, but it was something he felt he had to do, get it out of his system, as he put it. "I had read somewhere that if you have an addiction or some sort of obsession, one of the best ways to rid yourself of it was to overindulge until you got sick of it. Damn it. I'd tried everything else. I had nothing to lose."

Fleury smiled. "Sounds like wishful thinking," he said.

"Maybe," replied the other.

"Your wife thinks that if you left The Bahamas and returned to England you'd drink less."

"Davidson replied heatedly: "That's nonsense. My wife doesn't know what she's talking about. I can't leave here. I've got a job to do. I can't just throw it up like that."

"Your contract ends soon. You're not obliged to renew it."

There was a pause, then Davidson said he had nothing to go back to in England for.

"You can always find yourself another job."

Davidson gave a forced laugh. "You couldn't have said a less truer thing. Things just aren't like that. Once you've been abroad there's no return." He hesitated, but when Fleury was silent went on: "If I went back to England do you think anybody would want me? No, not on your life. They'd tell me that my experience wasn't any use to them; that I didn't fit in; that they couldn't possibly pay me what I was getting abroad. Then they'd be suspicious of a man who gave up a £5,000 a year job for a £2,000 one. It wouldn't make sense to them. They'd think I was crazy. And I'm not sure they wouldn't be right. Here, I've got a fine house, two cars, servants, everything I want. I've even been thinking of buying a yacht. In England I'd be a pauper. I'd hate myself if I depended on the family's money. On the other hand if I relied on my own earning power, I'd have to wait until I was nearly fifty to afford the things I want. England is out of the question. I've explained that to my wife a hundred times." He stopped abruptly and then, as though he had said something he hadn't intended to, avoided the doctor's gaze.

Fleury remained silent, but he noticed that Davidson's hands were shaking and he concluded that, at least on the subject of Nassau he felt strongly. Eventually Fleury said: "Your wife thinks that your health and your relationship with her are more important than anything else."

Davidson threw the doctor an angry glance. There was a long pause and then, as though resigned to fate, he acknowledged that drink was the problem, that he couldn't help himself and that he couldn't face the stuffy inhibiting atmosphere of his own or his wife's family. "At least here I've got a decent job. I can retain some self-respect. It means a lot to me that I am earning a good living and can keep both of us in a style of life we have been more or less accustomed to. Here I can keep off the wagon for long spells. In England I doubt if I could remain sober for a day."

The doctor looked at his watch and smiled. "The best thing you can do now is to go home and have some dinner. You've already exceeded your hour." He rose and showed the patient out.

The months rolled by. Davidson saw Fleury three times a week. It was nearly four months since his first visit. If the doctor had been optimistic at the beginning there were now only grounds for pessimism. Progress was slow or non-existent. The sessions were repetitive and monotonous. Little new material came to light. The doctor learnt that Davidson first started drinking in West Africa. Apparently, at the time he was having a lot of headaches, due to tension he thought, and that's why he began to drink: it relaxed him, he said; made him feel less inhibited, less self-centered. He realized he was drinking too much and began asking himself a lot of questions. In his spare time he read a lot about religion, especially Catholicism. He seemed to think that he needed to believe in something. His scientific training, however, made that difficult. Then he read *Varieties of Religious Experience* and that had been an eye-opener. William James' had had similar struggles with himself over the dilemma of free-will and predestination. Eventually he resolved the problem by making his first act of will to believe in free-will. Davidson decided to do the same with Catholicism. Faith would grow, he determined, the more he followed the rituals, doctrines and dogma of the

Church. He explained that when he believed something his headaches vanished or anyway diminished. They came back and with them the drinking, when he was assailed with doubts

Of course Fleury learnt much more about his patient—his likes and dislikes in books, movies, his food preferences, his views of women, prostitution, homosexuality and much more. Davidson claimed that he had had a homosexual experience at school, had never frequented a prostitute and had had his first sexual encounter with a barmaid when he was up at Cambridge. He had never been unfaithful to his wife. He loved her and didn't want to hurt her. He said he wanted to stop drinking but couldn't.

Fleury had a suspicion that Davidson had had some traumatic experience in West Africa, or (more to the point) that latent conflicts, character defects or weaknesses had been brought to the fore by some untoward event. Certainly, when talking about his experiences in Africa he was vague and appeared agitated, his eyes unable to focus, his hands clenched, his lips quivering and he even had a little stutter. When he spoke he simply described the day's routine. As for what he did in his spare time he said he played darts in the mess, sat around drinking with the boys, sometimes he played bridge, but really it was too hot to do anything other than sit around. There were no women other than native ones and he certainly hadn't fraternized with them, he said. The impression that Davidson wanted to give the doctor, it seemed, was that he had led a perfectly normal existence under trying circumstances. Fleury, however, wasn't quite convinced. He felt that his patient, away from the inhibiting influence of the family, especially his father, had perhaps had a sense of freedom that he had never experienced before, and had consequently let himself go and had indulged in a variety of new sensations. Was Davidson being honest, Fleury wondered? He had been very emphatic about his not fraternizing with the native women. He had been just as assertive in his denials of taking drugs, other than liquor. But what struck Fleury was that when Davidson returned to

England he became a Catholic; he stopped drinking for a while; he threw himself into his work; he gave himself few if any pleasures. It seemed as though he went from one extreme to another—a sort of reaction, the doctor thought, to what had been happening in Africa.

In connection with this Fleury was pleased that he had noticed something strange about Davidson at one of the cocktail parties. At the time he had observed that Davidson shied off expressing opinions. It was as though he was frightened of revealing a secret. His patient, now that he knew him better, only saw the world in black and white. He was either blatantly opinionated or awkward and retiring. Fleury got the impression that he was dogmatic with subordinates and social inferiors, but accommodating and humble with strangers and superiors. The doctor did not think much of Davidson as a man though he had no doubt of his intellectual prowess. Somehow he sensed that his patient knew that as a human being he was a failure, or at least inadequate in the image he had built for himself, and this was the real reason for his wanting to remain abroad. Out of England, particularly in a place like The Bahamas, a white man, propertied, educated and with good breeding, was a man to be reckoned with. It mattered little whether as a human being he was somewhat lacking. Such were some of the reflections that Fleury turned over in his mind as he sat listening to his patient.

Towards the end of the session Fleury told Davidson that things were not progressing as he had hoped and he intended, of course, with permission, to perhaps speed things up. He then suggested that a series of some half dozen intra-veinal injections might do the trick. Sodium Pentathol was the drug he proposed to use and this, he explained, was a kind of truth drug which would enable him to speak more freely, without feeling guilt and consequently help him penetrate deeper layers of the unconscious. The drug had no side effects and was quite harmless. It would, however, involve a change in his analytical schedule. Two sessions would be required each week—a two hour one for the Pentathol, followed by a one hour meeting to go through the findings of the previous occasion.

Davidson asked the doctor a few questions about the injections, then agreed to give them a try.

When he arrived the following week the atmosphere in the room was different. The blinds were drawn; the air-conditioning was off, though it was hot; a couple of blankets lay across the desk; on a small folding table next to the couch were a few antiseptic looking oddments—a syringe, a bottle of alcohol, cotton wool, rubber bands, two small boxes, a glass and tumbler. The doctor, as was his custom at the beginning of every session, asked if anything had happened since their last meeting.

"Nothing," answered the other.

"Well, we might as well start," replied the doctor. Then he asked Davidson to remove his shoes and shirt and lie on the couch. The drug was administered in two stages: the first induced drowsiness and sleep and the second stimulated the mind and produced a free flow of ideas. After Fleury removed the needle he covered Davidson with a blanket, for it was not unusual for the patient to feel cold.

The doctor pulled up a chair and seated himself in front of the couch. He watched the crinkles of anxiety iron themselves out from Davidson's face. The man seemed to turn into a young boy without worries or responsibilities.

"Tell me about Africa," said the doctor.

At first Davidson did not reply, but merely stared unblinkingly at the doctor. Then he smiled and his eyes seemed to soften: "You look like a very kind man," he said eventually. "Everything looks different. I feel good. Somehow nothing seems to matter. I don't feel threatened. I feel I could talk my head off and, say whatever I wanted and it wouldn't matter. My head is very clear."

"Tell me about Africa," Fleury repeated.

27

"Africa?... A lot happened there." He paused, the smile vanished and it struck the doctor a flicker of fear registered in the patient's eyes. "I haven't told a living soul." continued Davidson. "Not even my father confessor. I was too ashamed. Ever since I started coming to you I've been thinking about Africa. I thought of telling you everything, but I just couldn't. Now, with this stuff you've given me it doesn't seem so bad." Then he sat up abruptly; he was trembling; he looked around as though he had to protect himself from something. "There's something else," he said. "I don't know what it is, but I feel terrible."

"Are you feeling cold?" Fleury asked.

"I'm all right."

"Tell me what happened in Africa," the doctor gently encouraged.

Davidson was now lying down again. He hesitated then replied: "I fell madly in love. Head over heals in love. I'd never been in love before. I'd always been a self-centered sort of person and didn't think love, anyway for me, was possible. It hit me like a tornado. I felt helpless. I didn't know what was happening to me. All I knew was that I was prepared to do anything for my lover. I was prepared to die. I mean it. " Then he blurted it out: "I fell in love with a man."

For a moment there was silence. Fleury registered no emotion. He continued to stare at the prostrate figure.

Davidson continued: "It was a terrible shock to me. I'd never suspected such a tendency in me. I wasn't particularly attracted to girls, but I didn't dislike them. I liked the company of the boys, but nothing more than that, at least so I thought. At first I tried desperately to fight what I was feeling. No good. It was as though some power greater than me held me in a clamp. I was torn between agonies of guilt, shame and that I wasn't normal. With my background I felt an outcast. I just couldn't tell anybody. Then, I could have been thrown out of the army. How could I explain that to the family? I started to drink. I drunk much too much. On my days off I drunk myself silly. I practically got court-martialed. My behavior was disgraceful. If my lover hadn't been very thoughtful and considerate as well as being able to afford to go to a place out of town I would have been in deep trouble. He was married himself and his love for me was just as much a shock to him. Fortunately he had a good job with one of the big oil companies and we could go to this place in the suburbs. We both suffered agonies of guilt. We drowned ourselves with self-pity. We tried not to see each other. It didn't work. We were attracted to each other like magnets.

"`I'm not normal. I'm not normal'," I kept telling myself. " I wanted to sleep with the native women just to prove to myself that there was nothing wrong with me. I couldn't do it. I just got drunk instead. It was around this time that some Catholic literature came my way. I read vociferously. I exerted every ounce of will-power I was capable of. I avoided my beloved and every time I wanted a drink I had a cold shower. I had a lot of cold showers. My friends in the mess thought I was mad, as though I had some sort of compulsion like people who need to keep washing their hands. Gradually, however, my desires seemed to abate, or perhaps I was simply too exhausted to feel anything. I don't know. A couple of months passed without incident and I was sent back to England, shortly afterwards to be demobbed.

"My experience had shaken me and I was still frightened that I might have a repeat occurrence. I resolved to leave nothing to chance. I decided to become a Catholic and get married as soon as possible. A friend of mine at the time (I'd known him at school) asked me a lot of awkward questions. Did I believe in birth control, abortion, capital punishment? What about the infallibility of the Pope? And what did I think of censorship, the Inquisition and did I really think that non-Catholics would suffer eternal damnation? His questions troubled me. I had doubts and I would feel myself weakening. The only thing I could think of to tell him was that with reason you could prove anything. Or nothing. What really mattered, I said, was faith, and since I hadn't been fortunate enough to be given one, gratuitously, so to speak, I proposed to adopt one." Davidson stopped and became more agitated.

"Do you know what that bastard then told me?" he cried.

The doctor was silent.

The other went on: "He told me I was not only a fool but a coward as well. He said I wanted to become a Catholic to avoid the responsibilities of thinking for myself and making my own decisions. The difference between men of character and the rabble, he said, was that the former thought for themselves and the latter did what I was doing. `Of course,' he added `it 's a free country and you can do what you like'."

The patient had been excited in expressing these ideas. Now he calmed down. The doctor suspected that an emotional nerve had been touched. Davidson continued: "That was not all. He said it was absurd for me to get married at the present moment. If I did my marriage would end on the rocks. I was not going into marriage in a healthy frame of mind, but was using it, like Catholicism, as a prop. I tried to defend my position. I talked about stability, regular habits, somebody to help me and more. He listened, but when I had finished told me I was talking rot."

"A very outspoken friend," said Fleury quietly.

"Well, needless to say that ended our friendship. I didn't take his advice. In fact I did everything he thought I shouldn't do. I soon found the girl I was looking for. She was from a good family, Catholic, homely. She was attractive and tall with a boyish look, short hair and a warm friendly smile. I liked her though I didn't love her. Well, not in the sense of the all consuming passion I'd experienced in Africa. She was eminently suitable, I thought. She was a bright girl. She had a degree in English from Oxford and was an assistant to a newspaper counselor who had a column in the paper. It struck me that I was hardly likely to fall in love with a woman so I would do the best I could. You might say that my marriage was an arranged one. Arranged by me. And the funny thing about it, like so many arranged marriages, is that today I love my wife. At least in so far as I am capable of loving. She's been wonderful for me and I don't know what I would have done without her. Of course when we first got married I hoped that my affliction would go, that it was just

30

a passing phase.

"Unfortunately it didn't turn out that way. Against my will I began to make her life a misery. I cared for her deeply, but inner forces were pulling me in another direction. I began to drink again. I tried to stop. I saw experts, went in for various cures. No good. Drink was the only thing that took me out of myself, alleviated my headaches, made me forget. My drinking increased. When I finally realized the direction I was heading I wanted to get away from it all. I didn't want to disgrace the family. I decided that I had to go abroad. Of course I knew the family would get to know about me but distance, I felt, would blur their impressions. Actually, I wanted to get away from the family because I thought it would only exacerbate my guilt. Dorothy, like the good wife she is, didn't protest. Anyway, that's how we got to The Bahamas.

"The only bone of contention in all this was Dorothy. I had an inkling of what was in store for me and yet I had to deceive her shamefully. It did strike me that perhaps the honorable thing to do was to just slip away alone and give her the chance of beginning a new life. But I knew that wouldn't work either. She loved me. Divorce wasn't possible. She believed that she had to stand by me for better or for worse. Besides I needed her. She was clever at covering things up. Few people really knew what a state I was in. Without her I'm sure I would have gone to pieces completely. As it was I gave the appearance of functioning fairly well. My drinking is mostly solitary. I go to work more or less regularly and when I don't Dorothy covers up for me quite successfully."

Fleury cut in: "Have you told her about your experience in Africa?"

"No... I didn't dare. I was ashamed. Then with her background I felt she wouldn't understand. I hoped that the whole experience was just a passing phase and I'd got it out of my system."

The end of the session was approaching. Fleury gave the patient a sedative and a little while later dismissed him.

The third Pentathol session proved to be a little more revealing than the first. The doctor sensed that something more had happened in Africa than had been revealed. The previous session was mostly repetitive, but when the doctor probed into the relationship of his patient's lover he became agitated and switched to talking about something else. Fleury learnt that the love affair had lasted a few months. Both men were attracted to each other like flies to flypaper. Yet all the while they were together they suffered excruciating agonies of guilt, remorse, self-pity and were almost constantly rowing. Their backgrounds had a lot in common and neither could accept what had happened. They berated each other as well as themselves. It struck the doctor that the two men had more in common than just their backgrounds, for Davidson's lover would not tell his wife about the affair either. He loved her, he claimed, and went to considerable length arranging and concealing their clandestine meetings. When the doctor asked how they finally broke up Davidson seemed to get even more tense, his facial muscles tightened, he compressed his lips, he clenched his fists. It was as though he was using every ounce of energy to suppress the effect of the drug. In the end he would quite blandly reply that they just stopped seeing each other.

"That's it?" said the doctor and it flashed through his mind that his patient had perhaps killed his lover.

"Shortly afterwards I returned to England," said Davidson.

"Did you ever write to him?"

"Never."

"What happened to him?"

"I'm not sure."

"Does that mean you don't want to tell me?"

That was as far as the session got. No amount of indirect probing changed things. It struck Fleury that perhaps Davidson had hidden what had happened even from himself. Maybe he had fallen in love with a native boy and if he had vanished there wouldn't be too much probing.

The doctor decided that he must stop fantasying. "Did you ever say good-bye to each other?" he asked.

Davidson replied that they said their goodbyes every time they parted. They swore that it would be better for both of them if they didn't see each other. "Then one day," he said, "It really was a final good-bye."

In the drug free session that followed Fleury sought to persuade his patient that what he feared most probably wouldn't happen. He suggested that the drinking only occurred because he was frightened of falling in love again—with a man. That was hardly likely, he explained. Most adolescents went through a homosexual phase. Usually it didn't last long, especially when there were girls around. Davidson, continued Fleury, was a late developer and in many senses his military service was merely an extension of Public School. There was no reason, now that he was married and from all appearances happily so, that he hadn't got over that difficult phase in his life. If he stopped drinking he would probably learn that for himself. The only thing he had to fear was his own fear. Davidson was adamant. Nothing could convince him that if he stopped drinking the other thing wouldn't return. "Besides," he added, "I can't help myself. I can hold off for a while and then I go back again."

There was no doubt in the doctor's mind that little or no progress was being made. He knew also that his patient was aware of this. Davidson explained that the only reason he continued to see the doctor was because his wife wanted him to. Fleury, to some extent, thought otherwise. Davidson had become dependent on him; he also probably imagined that the therapy was his last hope. Or maybe the weekly visits had simply become routine, a reassuring habit which gave his schedule structure? But the doctor was an honest man. He did not believe, though he was qualified psychoanalyst, that patients should see him indefinitely. If a patient, after a while, wasn't improving he felt it right to tell him or her straight that he couldn't do any more, that perhaps help should be sought elsewhere. Doctor Fleury thought he hadn't quite reached this stage. An idea had kept working at the back of his mind.

The chances of its success were perhaps remote, but it might be worth a try.

"I've been giving a lot of thought to your particular case," he said when an opportune moment arose. "I don't profess to understand all that's happening. I'm not even sure you have told me all there is to know. Maybe there are certain things you are not even aware of yourself? Usually Pentathol opens a patient up. He feels free, unburdened by consequences and able to confess everything that is on his mind. In your case I feel there is something more. I don't know what it is and I could be wrong. My feeling is that if you could accept your past, and stop denying it as you are doing, you would feel an immense sense of relief, a release, so to speak, from your immense sense of guilt and feeling of inadequacy." The doctor paused and then went on: "What I want you to do is to tell your wife everything."

Fleury had no time to elaborate. The words acted on David like tonic. He went into a cold sweat. He became very white. His lips quivered and he began to shake. Eventually he replied feebly. "I can't do it. I won't do it. I'd rather die."

Silence.

A few moments passed. Gradually Davidson regained his composure. "I can't possibly do what you ask," he repeated and looked down at the floor.

The doctor continued: "The therapeutic value of confession is immense. Didn't you tell me yourself that you felt much better after going to confession? When you stopped going you told me you drank more. The same when you were going to Alcoholics Anonymous you said. Coming here, unburdening yourself to me, is also confession and you say you are drinking a little less now. I'm sure your wife would be very understanding. She loves you, you've said so yourself. She wants you to get better, I know. Having had a homosexual experience isn't the end of the world. Nor does it mean that you are one. You've said yourself that physically you get on fine with your wife. We all have two lives—an inner one and an outer one The extent that they are out of harmony with each other is the measure of our inability to cope. I want you to speak to your wife honestly because I think it would narrow the gap between the Jekyll and Hyde within you."

"I am drinking less now. No doubt about it. But I feel that if I stop seeing you my drinking would start again in earnest. As for speaking to my wife there's more to it than you imply. I'd have to tell her why I became a Catholic, why I married her and that I never really loved her. I just couldn't do it. It would break her heart."

"Don't you think that you're doing that already?"

Davidson did not reply at once and when he did he didn't quite answer the question. "She'd leave me. .. I'm sure of it."

"Don't you think she might anyway?"

"I don't know. At the moment she thinks she can pull me through."

"She wants children,"said Fleury.

Davidson laughed. "That might be one way to make her stick with me."

"Why are you still coming here?" asked the doctor.

"Frankly I don't know. I suppose it's because Dorothy wants me to continue seeing you."

"And you wouldn't if it wasn't for her?"

"I'm not sure; but probably not."

"You want to please her and yet you're not prepared to be fully honest with her?"

"I won't tell her what happened and that's final."

"I don't think I can help you," replied Fleury. "Maybe it would be better if I stopped seeing you?"

Davidson then flew into a rage and accused the doctor of wanting to get rid of him after he'd robbed him of a large chunk of money.

Fleury replied calmly as though the outburst had had no effect on him: "You are free to continue seeing me, or to stop. The choice is

35

yours. I'll always do my best to help you."

The young man gave the doctor a supplicating look. "I want to get better. I want to lead a normal life. I want children. I want to make my wife happy."

Fleury scratched his chin. "There's one more thing I could try," he said. "Come back at the usual time next week. Don't drink any alcohol for at least 24 hours before. I trust you can do that?"

And so, yet another session ended.

It was Friday evening and nearly 8:00 o'clock. Fleury sat in his chair head in his hands, waiting for Davidson. He had received an urgent call from him that morning at the hospital. Davidson had sounded terrible and had begged to see the doctor immediately. Fleury said that that was not possible, but he would see him that evening.

When Davidson arrived he staggered into the room and groped for support on the desk. His eyes were bleary and he looked disheveled. Part of his shirt was hanging out. His hair was a mess. About him was an air of agitation. He thanked the doctor for seeing him at such short notice. He apologized for the inconvenience he had caused. Then, seating himself in the chair facing the desk, he came straight to the point: "My wife's leaving me. She says she's going back to England whether I like it or not. She went to the doctor this morning and he confirmed that she was expecting. She didn't want to have her baby in Nassau. She dislikes it here. She thinks the place aggravates my troubles. Too many people drink here, she says. Liquor is too cheap. She claims I can get all the care I need in England. Then she believes that the feelings she's experiencing will do harm to the baby. She seems to have resigned herself that seeing you isn't doing much good. She wants to leave before my contract expires. I can follow her, she says. She's positive she won't return. She insists she still loves me; but now she has the baby to think of. I too, she tells me, as a father, have duties and responsibilities. She'll do everything to help me, she assures me, but won't compromise the baby."

Doctor Fleury slipped a pill into the glass on his desk and poured some water into it from the tumbler. "Drink this," he said. "It should help calm you down."

He gulped it down.

There was a pause.

"What do you want me to do?" asked the doctor.

"I want you to tell Dorothy that I am in the middle of my treatment: it would do more harm than good if I broke off now."

"I thought you said that she approved of you completing your contract? You've still got a few months haven't you?"

"I need her. I think if she wasn't here I'd drink a good deal more. I'd skip work more often. I might be sacked, or forced to resign. I'd never be able to stay on or return, even if I did have a spell in England."

"Have you spoken to her about what we discussed last time?"

"No."

There was a long pause and then the doctor repeated what he had said before. "In today's world the stigma of homosexuality is not what it used to be. More and more men and women too for that matter, are coming out of the closet. I am not saying at all that you are that way inclined. I think it very possible that your experience in Africa was an isolated incident. I believe your fears could be quite groundless. I think you really do love you wife. I think your drinking is, at least in part, due to an imaginary bugbear. Your situation is far from tragic. History is littered with famous people who have had a predilection for their own sex. I think it would relieve you immensely if you were to come out of the closet, so to speak. Let me rephrase that: I think you should tell your wife the truth because what happened to you is important to you; that does not mean that you are still that way inclined now. The closet in your case could simply be your prison."

"I don't think you understand my situation at all Doctor My

upbringing, my religion, my view of myself, my love for my wife—all make what you ask quite impossible. The only way I'd be able to make such a confession is if I was completely smashed. And if that was the case I don't think my wife would take me seriously."

"Why don't you try?" said the doctor.

Davidson was stunned by the reply. His face froze. He stared vacantly in front of him. He stopped clasping and unclasping his hands. He seemed to be at a complete loss for words.

"Well, what about it?"

Eventually the young man replied: "I'll go back to England. I'll try and persuade Dorothy to stay here as long as possible. We'll return together or I'll follow her very shortly afterwards. I'll stay in the UK a while. See how things go. If things work out that will be fine. If they don't I can always tell her the truth then. Or alternatively just return to Nassau on my own."

"In other words you want to delay making a decision?"

"I suppose you could put it that way."

Fleury felt there was nothing more to say, so he changed the subject and said he had had a long day; he was tired; he hadn't eaten yet and it seemed that nothing more would be gained by prolonging the session. He stood up as though this signaled the end of their meeting.

Davidson didn't budge. He sat vacantly staring in front of him. His hands were fidgeting again. Then he stood up and announced that he would tell his wife everything over the weekend.

The Monday arrived. It was a lovely day and as Fleury opened the blinds the sun poured into the room. He lingered for a few moments at the window. He stretched his arms and a feeling of well being passed through his body.

There was a knock on the door. "Come in."

The maid entered.

"Your breakfast is ready Sir."

"Thank you Mabel. I'll have it on the verandah this morning."

He slipped his dressing gown on and went out on the porch. As he sat down he threw the Nassau Guardian a quick glance.

"Good God," he gasped, shaken out of his calm. .

There, sprawled across the front page was the following headline: U.K. ENGINEER DROWNS AT LYFORD CAY.

Fleury quickly read the column. It said that Davidson, who was not a very good swimmer, had drowned the day before while at the beach with his wife and some friends. The circumstances of the case were not yet clear, but it seemed that he had got out of his depth, panicked and before anybody realized what was happening or could reach him it was too late. The column then went on to cite some of the deceased achievements. He was described as a young man with great promise, who came from a distinguished family, was highly qualified and had quickly gained a commission in Her Majesty's Forces. He had been serving with The Bahamas Light and Power Corporation for nearly three years and his service had been invaluable. Davidson, the article went on, was an honored and respected citizen in Nassau and his tragic untimely death would be a great loss to the community. He was survived by his wife. The funeral would be that afternoon.

The doctor read the column again more slowly. He felt distinctly sick. Primarily he felt dissatisfied with himself. He had failed. The thought that Davidson might commit suicide was not entirely unexpected. At the next session he had intended trying hypnotism. It struck him that perhaps his patient was hiding more than just a homosexual incident. He would never know. Still, he couldn't stop reproaching himself. He had handled the case badly. He had been too pushy about confession. Possibly it wouldn't have worked anyhow? Why did he think it would? Then it struck him that speculating on what he should or shouldn't have done accomplished nothing. He must look on the positive side: there was one.   Mrs Davidson would never know about her husband's experience in West Africa. She'd be able to return to England as she wanted. She'd be able to tell her child the good things about her husband. Then he remembered that she still loved him. He would call her and offer his condolences. He would attend the funeral. That was the least he could do. Still, he felt uncomfortable. Something kept telling him that it was all his fault. Then it struck him that perhaps he was being unfair to himself: maybe the whole thing really was an accident, exactly as the paper had described it?

The maid came in to clear away.

"Why Sir, you haven't touched your breakfast."

Fleury gave his oatmeal a jaundiced look. "No Mabel. I'm not feeling too well. Would you please call the hospital and say I won't be in this morning."

"Yes Sir."

Pearl

Going abroad, it is held, broadens the mind, is an education, helps you understand people and is invaluable experience for anything you might want to do. Rubbish. For most people travel means no more than lying on a beach (admittedly a foreign one), going to a good hotel, meeting people one sees at home and occasionally, for the more enterprising, visiting a museum, picture gallery or a church or two. The urge to travel is probably no more significant than the desire to be fashionable, escape from oneself or fill one's photograph album with hundreds of snaps. All this, however, did not apply to Alan Flabian, a shy slender young man of 23 with a long serious face, high forehead and plenty of black hair. He was in fact an aspiring writer. He was wearing a light blue shirt, white polyester trousers. A camera was strapped over his shoulder. He was well aware that traveling did not make a person a writer and he cited the Bronte sisters, Flaubert and others who had done practically no traveling and yet had distinguished themselves in the world of letters. When then, people asked him why he traveled he told them that for him it was necessary. It was what he had always wanted to do and, although he was conscious how lonely and dreary (as well as expensive) it could be, he thought it sacrilege not to pursue one's inner dreams and hopes. Thus, for the first time in his life he was going round the world. At present he was island hopping in the Caribbean. He fastened his seat belt and the little Heron from St. Thomas nosed its way down towards St. Kitts, northernmost island of the British West Indies.

St Kitts was like nothing Flabian had ever seen. Contrary to other West Indian islands it was almost untouched by tourists. The people lived mainly by agriculture with sugar cane the main crop. There was virtually no industry and the place seemed completely lifeless as the taxi made its way through the few deserted streets of Basseterre, capital of St. Kitts. Flabian was traveling on a budget and wanted somewhere cheap. The taxi driver took him to a few boarding houses, which weren't really boarding houses at all, but homes where occasional guests were taken in. The places looked so depressing that Flabian eventually told the driver to take him to the best hotel in town. This was The Palms and looked quite third rate. The hotel overlooked a square. There were no grounds, no fancy entrance: the structure was wooden and badly needed a coat of paint. Flabian paid the driver and climbed the steps to the foyer, a very plain looking affair with boarded floors, cheap tables and chairs, with the lobby extending to a verandah that overlooked the square where he had just arrived. There were two groups in the room and when he entered conversation froze and everybody stared at him. In the first group four men were at a table as though playing cards. Drinks were in their hands. There were seven or eight people in the other assemblage. They too were sipping drinks, but appeared more casual with their chairs haphazardly arranged around two tables. The talk quickly resumed and Flabian waited for somebody to attend to him.

"Join us for a drink," said one of the men in the smaller group.

"That's very kind of you, but I'd like to get settled in my room first."

"Sounds as though you're English?" continued the other. "Are you a traveling salesman?"

"No. I'm a writer," replied Flabian .

The man gave his friends a significant look. "A writer eh. What d'you write—thrillers?"

Flabian smiled. "I'm afraid not. Recently I've been concentrating on articles and short stories."

"Short stories eh?" the man gave a sinister chuckle. "I could tell you a story or two. You've come to just the right person." He threw his colleagues a sidelong glance.

Flabian, who had received hundreds of similar offers, politely said he'd love to hear some of them. The other stood up.

"I'm Captain Thomas." Then he introduced the others: "this is my first mate, Edmond Perez; second mate, Martin Jardin and Lewis Moore, my chief engineer and the only traitor amongst us."

Polite how-do-you-dos were exchanged and one of them explained that Moore was the only one who wasn't a bachelor.

The captain was a short pot bellied man with dark hair, plump red cheeks, brown eyes and a mop of unruly black hair. He said he was English too, born in Trinidad, but had run away from home when he was fourteen. He had been at sea ever since, now nearly fifteen years. It was a hard life, he said. It was lonely. 80 per cent of the time they were at sea with nothing to do. There were no women; they got bored with each other. They went to the same places again and again. He knew the islands like the taste of rum and coke. Still, he loved the life and wouldn't change it for anything. Now, he was the captain of a cargo ship. They carried pine-apple, copra, sugar cane, bananas or whatever between the islands. He said there were 22 men aboard his ship, most were from Trinidad and, except for himself and his first mate, were all black. His first mate, Perez, was of Lebanese origin and born in Dominica. Flabian took him to be about 30. He had a wiry look, swarthy complexion, black hair, brown eyes, and was about 5' 8". The writer got the impression that he was highly strung, for he was constantly looking around as though he had to avert some sort of danger. Apparently he had traveled the world over and had worked for many skippers. The other two men were very black with thick lips, high cheek bones, fuzzy hair. Both were tall and muscular and appeared as though they were used to hard work. Martin Jardin was born in Tobago and had a touch of Indian blood in him which it struck Flabian might have accounted for his long thin nose. He too had run away to sea when he was fourteen. Lewis Moore, the captain described, as an educated man as he had left school when he was seventeen. He was Jamaican. His wife was very lovely and he had a beautiful home just outside Kingston. Of the four, Thomas perhaps enviously observed, he was the only one who had some claim to respectability.

There was a pause, but before the skipper had time to say more the proprietress of the hotel arrived and Flabian attended to the more practical matters of registering and settling in his room. After a somewhat unsatisfactory lunch he returned to the lounge to find the cargo ship boys still at their table drinking.

"Don't you fellows ever eat?" he said pulling up a chair.

The captain winked. "Not when we're ashore. Time's too precious for that." And he cupped his hand affectionately round his glass. He went on more seriously: "You see I don't allow liquor on board. I don't want my men drunk when they should be working, and it would be wrong for the officers to drink if the men weren't allowed to."

"I suppose you play a lot of cards," said Flabian.

"No. Don't allow gambling on board either. Gambling starts rows and rows lead to disorder and mutiny and I'm not 'aving that on my ship."

"What do you do with your spare time then? You must find it quite a job to fill up."

Thomas shrugged. "We do. That's why we stop off at these islands now and again. We've got no cargo to load or unload here, but the boys were getting restless so I thought I'd give them a break. When the ship is in dock they can do what the 'ell they like. I don't give a damn as long as they don't get into trouble with the law. As far as I'm concerned they're only two things that interest me when I'm ashore: Women and liquor and in that order!"

Flabian gave a faint smile. "I shouldn't have thought St. Kitts was much of a place as far as women are concerned."

The skipper grinned. "It isn't, but we 'aven't been 'ere for eighteen months and I thought it might be a good idea to drop in and see if there were any new additions to the local talent. I'll be looking round the wharf tonight."

Perez cut in. "It shouldn't be too bad here tonight. Friday's dance night and with the Caribbean destroyer in port it should be quite a big affair. I'll be going to the dance even you aren't."

The captain gave his mate a wry look. "Not our type Edmond. We won't find the sort of girls we're looking for at a dance like that."

"Speak for yourself," cried Perez haughtily. "I know how to handle women. There's not much I don't know about women. I'll be prepared to bet you that before the night is out I'll have one in bed with me."

The skipper laughed. "Yeah. But I'm sure you won't 'ave picked her up at the dance. The only women you know anything about are whores."

"Whores are women," protested Perez. "I can manage one sort just as much as another. All women are the same."

Thomas shrugged. "'ave it your own way. But as far as I'm concerned there are only two types of women: nice women and whores; and I know which I prefers—whores."

He then went on addressing Flabian his words slightly slurred. "There's not much I don't know about whores. Whores and ships, those are my specialities. Now, if you're thinking of picking up a whore never go to a bar. A bar is a racket. You'll pay the earth to have a girl sit with you. She'll have one drink after another, water colored with tea. Then when the place closes, it's goodbye. She won't even give you a kiss. I know I've been caught by that game more than once. The best type of girl is the street walker and preferably one who is pretty and not too expensive. Pretty, because if she ain't there's not much point going with her; inexpensive as this is an indication that she thinks modestly of 'erself." Then he added as though it was an afterthought: "I'm sure with all that inside information you'll be able to make a jolly good story."

Flabian acknowledged that it could be useful background material.

Thomas continued: "You should see life a bit more. Why don't you become a sailor for a little while. There's not much a sailor don't know about life."

"Perhaps that's what I'll do," said Flabian. "At present I'm trying to get as much experience as possible as I think it will help with my work. Everything is grist for the mill."

"Tell you what," pursued the captain. "Why don't you join us on the wharf tonight and I'll introduce you to low life. If you're a writer you'll want to see some of that too."

"Yes, naturally but if there's a dance here I should prefer to go to that."

"Quite right," interjected Perez. "You don't want to get mixed up in a brawl with a lot of harlots. A respectable fellow like you should be able to find all he wants at the dance."

"Well, even if he does I'm sure you won't 'ave any such luck. The only woman you're going to seduce is a whore."

Perez, touched to the quick flashed angrily: "Bet."

The skipper laughed. "I don't want to take your money. You aint got a hope in 'ell. You would be as good as making me a gift".

"That's my look-out," cried Perez. "Two hundred bucks. Is it a deal?"

There was a pause, then the skipper put out a hand. "Done. But don't say I didn't warn you."

The technicalities were then thrashed out. The others would be witnesses. If by the time the ship lifted anchor Perez had not seduced a nice girl, as he put it, he would be out of pocket $200.

The chief engineer, the scholar in the group, then put forward a disturbing proposition: "How will we know if Edmond is telling the truth? He can say what he likes."

"I'll go to the woman direct and ask her," said the skipper.

"Moore smiled knowingly. "No respectable woman is going to admit to a lapse in her womanhood," he said.

There was a pause. "Let's call the whole thing off," said the captain.

"And lose the easiest way of making a quick two hundred bucks," smiled Perez. "Not on your life."

The others laughed. There was a pause. Eventually Thomas came out with an idea. "Tell you what Edmond. I'll take your word for it. Just before we leave we'll all meet for a drink and you can tell us what happened. These gentlemen will be your judges. If they think you are telling the truth I will pay without a murmur. Otherwise, or if you admit you 'aint been successful, you'll owe me a couple of hundred bucks. OK?"

Perez put out his hand.

"And do you guys agree to be the judges?" said Thomas.

The others nodded and they arranged to meet on the wharf Monday morning at 8:30. "We sail at 10:00," said the skipper and then he yelled to the barman. "John. Five more rum and cokes."

To Flabian the whole thing seemed ridiculous. But then it struck him these guys were macho. Their manhood was at stake. In a bygone age men fought duels for lesser issues. All part of his apprenticeship, he thought. He remained with the sailor boys drinking and chatting till about 5:00 at which time they left to go aboard for their evening meal.

The dance started at 9:30 and Flabian, after dinner and a short rest, had changed into a dark suit. He made his appearance in the lounge just after 10:00 and by this time the dance was in full swing. For a moment he stood and surveyed the scene. The center of the room had been cleared of tables and chairs and these had been pushed to the sides and onto the verandah. A steel band in one corner was playing a Calypso. The floor was packed. Many stood around the sides chatting. But what impressed Flabian was the hybrid nature of the people in the room. Here was democracy at its best, he thought. You saw a strange cocktail of rich and poor, White and Black, educated and uneducated, the small and the great, everybody in fact—all thrown together like a fruit cocktail. At the dance you saw humble sailors, neat and all in white; the Commodore of the Caribbean, the Captain of the destroyer in navy blue suits with decorative ribbons on theirs chests, many distinguished Kittitians, some of the cargo ship boys (casual looking, though neater than earlier), traveling salesmen and a score of nobodies. The women wore light and colorful dresses. All these people chatted together, patted each other on the back, bought drinks for one another, danced with the same women and showed the incredulous Flabian, by nature somewhat cynical, that different peoples, racially and culturally, could happily mix together, anyway for a short time. After gaping at this scene for a while Flabian went and found himself a dancing partner, an attractive young woman in a yellow and red polka dress. He was quite expert at this sort of dancing and they shuffled away as she fixed a frozen smile and a wide-eyed stare on him as though he was the most important person in the world. In due course the music stopped and Flabian joined the skipper who was sitting in a corner alone, sprawled in a chair, flushed as though partly inebriated.

"Whot'll you 'ave?" he greeted the writer.

"Rum and coke please, but the next one is on me."

The captain waved the remark aside and yelled for John to bring two rum and cokes. He paused and after two loud belches said: "oo's that woman you were dancing with. I know 'er from somewhere. Damn nice piece of work."

Flabian said she was the wife of one of the local magistrates. She was Cuban and had only recently got married. She had just got out of her country in time and managed to escape the worst of the Fidel Castro purges. At the time the magistrate had been vacationing in Havana. It was love at first sight apparently. Anyway, he managed to get her into St. Kitts and it wasn't long before they married.

The barman served them their drinks.

"And what's 'er name?" asked Thomas.

"I forget her surname, but her christian name is Pearl."

"Perla?"

"I suppose that's what it would be in Spanish."

The skipper took a gulp at his drink and nodded his head approvingly. "Damn nice piece of work. I admire your taste. I think I'll 'ave a bash at 'er myself." He got up and went and hung around her chair waiting for the music to start.

Now, however, crudely the captain might express himself what he said was true. Pearl was uncommonly beautiful. She was of medium height, slender with a fine waist line and perky breasts, not too large. If her figure was good her face was stunning. It was long, majestic with classically chiseled features: high cheek bones, a little pointed chin, soft sensual lips and those hypnotic eyes which gazed at you as though you were all that mattered. But what had impressed Flabian even more was the texture of her skin. It was pale and white with only a touch of color on the cheeks and very smooth like the skin of a baby. Flabian had dabbled in physiognomy and it amused him to speculate on the relationship between character and beauty. It struck him that the two were basically incompatible. Character implied experience, effort, hardship of some kind and this he thought showed itself on the face. There were wrinkles of worry, the beginnings of furrows on the brow, lines of effort round the mouth, some sort of a kink that spoilt a perfectly symmetrical look. Pearl, Flabian conjectured, had the face of a woman who had never struggled and probably had accepted the wealth, position and ease of the class she had been born into without much thought. Thus the young writer sat sipping his drink, looking on, absorbing the atmosphere in the room and now and again throwing the skipper a glance to see how he was doing.

The music started up again and Thomas asked Pearl to dance. She excused herself and got up to dance with the Commodore. The skipper lingered a few moments then rejoined Flabian.

"No luck?" the writer smiled

Skipper Thomas grunted. "She said she'd promised the dance to somebody else."

"Oh well. The evening is young. You've got plenty of time."

The captain belched.

"She's certainly something!" he went on. "She's even better looking close up. She's about the prettiest piece of fluff I've ever seen.'

"Do you know her?"

"Now wheres would I knows a thing like that from? I don't know any aristocracy, even Cuban aristocracy."

"Anyway, are you pleased you came to the dance?"

The skipper pondered a moment. "I don't know that I am, now you comes to ask me. It frustrates a man to see all that beauty gone to waste. I think I'll slip out and have a look around the wharf a little later."

More drinks were ordered. There was a pause and Thomas prodded Flabian in the groin. "Tell you what. You're a writer. You want a bit of experience don't you? How about coming on my ship for a bit? I'll sign you up as a member of the crew."

"That's very kind of you but I intend to go south. If you're going to Trinidad I should be very glad for a lift."

"Sure. Take you as far south as George Town if you like. We'll stop over at some of the islands and you can look around them. You don't mind doing a spot of painting do you?"

"Not at all. Is that all I'll have to do?"

Thomas shrugged. "Oh, there's not much to do, but it won't be like one of them luxury 'olidays. It's no Mediterranean cruise you'll be on and it'll be up to you 'ow you gets on with the boys. I won't meddle on your behalf."

Alan Flabian played for time. "I don't think that would worry me, but I'm ever such a bad sailor. Is it rough? I wouldn't want to spend the whole time on my bunk."

The captain laughed. "Bunk! You don't get no bunk. You sleep in a 'ammock. Anyway, this time of year aint too bad. The 'urricane season is over."

"Is there anything special I'd have to bring with me?"

Thomas hesitated then answered: " There're two things I always keeps at the side of my 'ammock at night: a torch and a knife. Darkness creates panic. You fall over things. You grope. You get muddled. A torch prevents that." He took a swill at his drink then continued: "On a boat there's always lots of wires and ropes. If anything gets stuck all you 'ave to do is slash away. There may be a life-boat which has got caught in some ropes. With a knife you can cut it and the boat drops to the water."

"I think I'll be able to get myself a torch and knife, even in St Kitts."

Thomas put his hand round Flabian's shoulder and gave him an affectionate pat. "I like you. I want you to come with us, but I'd like you to talk to Edmond first. 'e'll be able to give you a better idea of what there is to do. I'll speak to 'im about you when I see 'im."

"He's not very far," said Flabian. "He's dancing with Pearl."

The captain looked up abruptly. "My God, so 'e is. The old rascal." He winked and looked at the writer closely giving him a whiff of his unwholesome breath. "If he thinks 'e's going to get anywhere with 'er 'e's a bigger dreamer than I thought 'e was."

"He doesn't seem to be doing too badly," said Flabian.

The skipper summarily dismissed the remark. "Bah! That's nothing. The women get bored 'ere. They like a bit of a flirt now and again. But they don't let you get very far. They're a frustrating lot of 'ussies these Kittitians."

"Anyway, I don't expect her 'usband is very far. He'll probably appear from nowhere if she begins making a fool of 'erself. I wonder where he is?"

"Probably in bed and asleep ," answered the skipper. "'e's probably fifty years older than 'er and wouldn't miss his night's sleep for anything."

"If I had a pretty little wife like that I wouldn't want her out of my sight for long," said Flabian.

For a few moments they just sat, drinking, watching the dancing. When the music stopped Perez joined them. He now looked quite dashing. He had shaved and smelt of aftershave, his hair was greased back. He wore a blue suit and white open shirt.

"If you think you're going to get anywhere with that tomato you're dreamin," Thomas said.

"She's a very beautiful woman," acknowledge Perez.

The skipper, grinning mischievously, went on: "Now you watch your step my man. I don't want any troubles with the law. You keep off that tomato otherwise you'll 'ave an angry 'usband on your tail."

Perez smiled. "He's away in Anguilla. He's on one of his circuits and won't be back until the end of next week."

The skipped gave a little laugh which turned into a belch. "You old bastard. But it don't mean that because the boss is away she'll play. Your sights are too high old man. You won't get anywhere with 'er I can tell you that."

"Never said I wanted to," replied Perez. "You bet I wouldn't pick up a nice girl before we left. You never mentioned anything about a particular dame."

Thomas looked bewildered. "Don't you like 'er? You seemed to be getting along fine with 'er."

"How I was getting on with her is my business." Perez sat down and took a swill at his drink and you got the impression he didn't want to discuss the matter further.

Thomas felt a little shiver of satisfaction run down his spine. He wasn't an envious man, but it wouldn't have been human if he hadn't felt a pang of jealousy in the knowledge that his first mate was being successful in his efforts to seduce so beautiful a woman as Pearl. Their interchange, however, had dismissed all such qualms. He felt that if

Perez had been really getting on well with her he would have been at some pains to hide it and would not have been so eager to change the subject. It was then the skipper switched to talking about his proposition to the writer.

"You tell our friend 'ere what you think about it. Tell 'im what he wants to know. I'm going to try my luck with Pearl."

He rose and staggered towards the center of the lounge. Pearl was again dancing with the Commodore and the skipper hung around, chatting with this and that person, waiting for the music to stop.

Perez, after a short silence said: "You mustn't come with us. I don't know what George has been telling you, but I'm sure that whatever he said he didn't mean."

The writer threw the first mate a look of surprise. "What makes you say that? I got the impression he was quite sincere."

"Can't you see he's as high as hell. What he says today will be forgotten tomorrow."

This reply disconcerted the young writer. He wasn't sure whether the first mate was speaking the truth or had simply taken a dislike to him.

"Why d'you think I shouldn't come?" he asked.

"It's tough, that's why. You'll ruin your life. I know: I've been in it for sixteen years."

"In what way is it tough?"

"Chiefly the food and accommodation. It couldn't be worse."

"And what about the work?" pursued Flabian.

"Oh that's nothing. That's the least of your worries. You'll probably be bored most of the time."

"You think I shouldn't come then?"

"I think it would do you more harm than good. I've seen many fellows go to sea and it's never done them any good. Look at me. I'm a sentimentalist. I love music and children. I should far prefer to be settled with a wife, kids, a home, a decent job. Instead I've got nothing. For your own sake you mustn't come."

On that note the conversation ended and they both drank and watched the dancing.

The rest of the evening passed quickly. Flabian circulated and met a score of people. The officers of the destroyer, neat well spoken men, explained in a rather self-important way that they were on hurricane patrol. They were equipped with food, medical supplies, doctors and much else; they could at a moment's notice be dispatched to an island a thousand miles away. Sometimes, however, as was the case recently in Grenada, they were alerted because a general strike threatened and there was risk of revolution. They were armed and a handful of their men could easily crush any insurrection. They patrolled the Caribbean and gave help to whomsoever needed it. At present they were paying St Kitts a courtesy visit.

But no less interesting than the officers were the men. They spoke differently. Most of them were signed on for nine years and would never be officers. They explained that they hadn't the right background. In the Navy background was everything. If your father wasn't an admiral or something and you hadn't that Oxford accent you got nowhere. When the writer met the Captain and the Commodore he was half inclined to believe them, for both had impeccable Oxonian accents. The men talked of their life at sea, women and what they would do at the end of their nine years. They were a well behaved lot on the whole: they drank a good deal and a four letter word was frequently on their lips, but they were not argumentative and there were no brawls. All grist for the mill Flabian thought.

During the course of the evening he danced with Pearl several times. She was very interested to learn that he was an author. She said she loved reading and would have liked to write too, but what with one thing and another she hadn't the time. She asked him what he thought of St Kitts. He said he hadn't seen very much yet, but liked what he had seen so far. She then offered to lend him her car so he could tour the island. Sunday afternoon, she suggested. Sunday was always a dull day. The officers were having a party on the ship in the evening and probably wouldn't be ashore in the afternoon. She enquired if he was going. When he said he hadn't been invited she said she'd try and get him an invitation. Flabian felt flattered that so beautiful a woman could pay so much attention to him. This was only marred, he felt, by the fact that all the women were equally nice to him: none refused to dance with him; they were all pleasant and a few suggested that, if he was in the Colony long enough, he should come to their home for a meal. The women seemed to have no favorites. Pearl also appeared to be just as charming whether she was dancing with the Commodore or the lowliest sailor. Nor could the men have been more friendly. They invited strangers to drinks, chatted with people beneath them and husbands watched their wives dance with other men without any apparent rancor. Flabian was having the time of his life.

The dance was scheduled to end at 2:00 a.m., but an hour later the place was still packed and the band was going full Calypso. Flabian noticed that the skipper had slipped away just after 1:00, but Perez had remained and it did not escape the writer's attention, that he too had had his fair share of dances with the beauty of the evening. Pearl, it seemed had danced with everybody. Her energy appeared tireless and if she had shown any preference for a dancing partner it was perhaps the Commodore. But Flabian only noticed this because he had been watching her closely. The band finally packed up shortly before 4:00 a.m. Alan Flabian retired to bed a tired and happy man.

Next day he had a lazy morning and only got up shortly before 1:00. After he'd had lunch he wrote up his impressions of the previous evening and it wasn't until nearly 5:00 that he made his appearance in the lounge. The skipper, with rings under his eyes, baggy cheeks, looking none too happy, was having tea. For him this meant rum and coke..

"You're looking like the day after the night before,"Flabian said joining him at the table.

Thomas grunted and said that was precisely how he felt.

"I noticed you slip away from the dance," said Flabian. "What time did you get to bed?"

"Reckon it must 'ave been around 5:00. I thought I'd 'ave a look a round the wharf."

"Discover any new talent?"

The captain belched and shrugged. "None that I was interested in. To be quite honest I could only think of Pearl. He then said that after he had left the dance he had gone to a bar on the wharf. He had ordered himself a drink and the whores had hovered around him like moths attracted to a light. He wanted to pick one of the girls up, but couldn't stop thinking about Pearl. He had half a mind to return to the dance, but didn't as he thought that would make him even more frustrated. He lingered at the bar, hoping that Edmond or one of the other boys would join him. None did, so he went for a walk. When he heard the music stop at the hotel he returned to the bar convinced that the others would turn up, since they had nowhere else to go. As he went down one of the side streets he saw Pearl get into one of the cars. She was with a man, he didn't see properly, but he was prepared to swear it was the Commodore.

"I was wild I tell you. I even chased after the car a little. I would have killed the bugger. I knew 'e was a Commodore and all that, but I felt 'e 'ad no more rights than I did."

Flabian smiled faintly. "I expect you're making a mountain out of a molehill. It probably wasn't them at all. I'm sure that neither would want a scandal."

"Yeah. That's what I thought later, but it ain't what I thought at the time. At the time I could 'ave sworn it was them. Anyway, I 'urried along to the bar. I needed a drink bad and wanted to see Edmond. I wasn't 'alf shocked when 'e wasn't there. I began to think p'rhaps 'e'd picked up some woman at the dance as 'e said 'e would. I 'ung around waitin, expectin 'im to to turn up at any moment, but 'e didn't and around 5:00 I returned to the ship." He chuckled. "I needn't 'ave worried my 'ead off. There e' was, like a good little boy, fast asleep with 'is bottom bulgin in the 'ammock."

"Well, I gets myself into the 'ammock and tries to sleep. It was getting light, but I 'ad all day and there was no 'urry for me to get up. But could I sleep? Not on your life. I lay there dreamin of Pearl. I tried to distract myself by thinkin of all them beautiful whores. No good. It was always Pearl that I kept thinkin' about. I began to tell myself: `George you're in love'. Not a wink did I sleep. All day I've been thinkin' of 'er. I've been wonderin' what do to. Of course I've been in love before and I'm mighty passionate. I get mad if I can't get what I want. It's seeing the Commodore with 'er that really got me. It wouldn't 'ave been so bad if nobody could 'ave her. `George you stick to whores,' I said to myself: `It's no use goin' after what you can't get!'"

Flabian repeated what he had said before: It probably wasn't them as neither would want a scandal.

"Yeah. You're probably right, but it don't mean that I 'aven't been struck by 'er."

"Things are always more attractive if we can't have them," said the writer. "I don't suppose she'd interest you after you spent a night with her."

"I can't tell you that until after it 'appens," he grinned.

"You'll forget all about her once you're at sea again."

Thomas ordered some more drinks and Flabian changed the subject and asked where the others were.

"Dunno. I saw Edmond this morning, but I 'aven't seen Martin or

Lewis all day."

"Edmond told me last night that he wasn't too keen on my coming with you. He says he thinks it'll ruin my life."

The skipper waved the remark aside with a sweep of his arm, spilling a little of his drink. "'e told me what 'e said to you. But the offer still stands. I'm captain and I decide who comes and who don't."

Flabian thanked him and the skipper continued: " It 'aint necessary for you to give an answer right away. You think it over and let me know tomorrow."

There was silence. Flabian scrutinized the skipper. He looked particularly ugly, he thought. His cheeks were very red and bulged hideously as though he had just come from the dentist. His words were slurred. He was drooling a little. His eyes, bloodshot, had a distant look about them. His movements were awkward. It struck the writer that this man had been drinking solidly ever since his arrival, just about 36 hours ago. The guy was no more than a bum, Flabian reflected, but he seemed to be quite a decent fellow and maybe a short spell at sea would be an interesting and rewarding experience? It was while he was toying with what to do that Perez turned up..

"I thought I'd find you here," he greeted them and shook hands with Flabian. "How did you enjoy the dance?" he asked.

"Very much. It was quite an experience. Never seen anything like it."

"Drink up both of you, the next round is on me," said Perez and yelled for John to bring three more rum and cokes as well as some nuts and chips.

The skipper shifted his position and stared at his mate. "What's wrong with you Edmond? Sounds as though you're 'appy. You don't think you've won your bet do you?"

"I'll leave that for the judges to decide when we meet Monday morning. He then turned to Flabian. "Listen, I take back all I said last night. If you want to come with us you come. Don't mind what I said at the dance. I was p'raps exaggerating things."

"What has made you change your mind?" asked Flabian.

"Well, I was thinkin' things over. It can't do you much harm I thinks to myself. If you want to come why shouldn't you? After all it 'aint as though you was going to be with us for ever."

"That makes it much easier for me to make a decision."

"I've given 'im till tomorrow to decide," said the skipper.

John served them and they drank and nibbled in silence. Perez was leaning back in his chair and looked as though he hadn't a care in the world. His jaw and mouth were relaxed. His eyes were a little red and he looked slightly sleepy. Nevertheless, there was something about him which gave the writer the impression that he was on a high. Not drunk, but simply in good spirits. He looked neat like he did at the dance.. He was shaven, his hair was greased back and he had clean soapy odor about him. Flabian reflected that notwithstanding his small stature, his self-confessed sentimentality, he was a fine figure of a man with a silent toughness which he (Flabian) had little doubt was attractive to women. Women, the writer, had concluded were just as attracted by looks as men. Add to that, it had always struck him, that they liked self-confidence and decisiveness in a man. Perez, it seemed, had both, notwithstanding that he had just changed his mind about Flabian joining them at sea.

"Goddamit, that woman's done something to me," thundered the captain, as though he could not contain the pressure of thoughts that had been preoccupying him during their moments of silence. "I don't know what it is, but I never feels this way before. She fairly knocked the fun out of all them harlots last night. I couldn't 'ave touched one with a lamp post." He chuckled. "With 'ussies like 'er around I can see myself becoming a respectable 'usband and all that."

Perez gave a forced laugh. "That's what you said about that woman in Nicaragua. If we hadn't got you out of the place damn quick you'd 'ave done something very silly and married the wench. Thank God you can't do anything so foolish with Pearl."

"I can't get 'er out of my mind. I tell you Edmond she's got me by the balls. She's different to that bitch in Nicaragua."

Perez began laughing. He just went on and on. He rolled about in his chair.

"What the 'ell are you laughing at?" demanded the skipper angrily.

"You. You stand about as much chance with Pearl as you do with the Queen of England."

"You take that back," cried the other his pride now touched to the quick. "I know if I was 'ere a bit longer I could do what the 'ell I wanted with 'er."

"Balls," said Perez calming down a little but still laughing. "You're dreamin. If you were here for a month of Sundays it wouldn't make a drip of difference. Stop kiddin yourself."

The skipper then did a very foolish thing. "Bet," he cried.

"Sure," replied Perez, his eyes sparkling and his hand outstretched.

"Two hundred bucks" said the skipper.

"I don't want to take your money George. You can still change your mind. It 'aint a deal until we shake on it."

"The same arrangement as for you," said Thomas grabbing his mate's hand. Just one thing more. We stay in St Kitts 24 hours longer. We leave on Tuesday."

"You think you'll have a better chance when the Commodore 'as gone?"

"It'll give you another day too," said the skipper as though he was pressing a bribe.

"What makes you think I'll need another day?"

"Shake on it," said the skipper as though he didn't want to discuss the matter further. Flabian got the impression that he would have liked to call the whole thing off, but didn't because he was too proud to admit that he had been foolish. He got up and staggered out of the lounge.

When he was out of earshot Perez, smiling and with a self-satisfied air, leaned over and whispered in the writer's ear. "This time I've got him. He thinks he'll get a chance Monday night. He won't. He doesn't stand a hope in hell. It's me that will be with Pearl Monday night. Sure as pie. Why d'you think I didn't kick when he wanted to stay an extra day? I'm gonna win four hundred bucks."

Flabian kept silent. He was a little shocked however. He wondered whether Perez was lying, boasting or simply trying to pull a fast one over him—getting the writer to be supportive when confronted by judgment time, just before leaving. He didn't know what to think. The skipper was only away a couple of minutes and now returned. A little later Flabian retired to his room.

Sunday afternoon arrived and immediately after lunch Flabian set out for Pearl's house. It was a little way out of Basseterre and was about a twenty five minute walk. She had told him the car would be outside the house and the key under the front door mat. There was no particular hurry. She didn't need the car before 6:00. The petrol tank would be full. The car had recently been serviced. The breaks worked fine. There was nothing to worry about. She recommended he see the Black Rocks and Brimstone Hill. On his return he should leave the car where he had found it and put the key back under the mat. No other instructions and no explanations as to where she would be. When he arrived, however, there was no car in front of the house and only dust under the mat. Just as he was about to ring the front door bell it opened and she was standing there.

"I zought I saw you arrive," she smiled. "I have decided to come with you. It is a beautiful afternoon and I zought perhaps you would like me as your guide?"

"I should love it, but really I don't want to take you away from anything if you are busy. As it is you are being more than kind."

She dismissed his remark with a dainty shrug. "Noseeng at all. It amuses me to show people little St Kitts. I shall have time for a siesta before de party tonight." She was holding some keys which she gave to him. "De car is in de garage. You drive and I shall be your guide."

Soon they were speeding out towards the Black Rocks. Pearl didn't exactly know where they were. She had a terrible head for directions, she said; but she would recognize the turning when she saw it. As he drove, his eyes on the rickety road, looking at the pleasant green hillocks here and there and in the distance, she kept up an incessant jabber. She spoke about the dance. She thought the Commodore very funny with his English accent. Some of the officers too, she went on, were very good looking and the sailors amused her with their funny and suggestive tattoos down their arms. St Kitts, she explained, was a dull place. There was nothing to do. The men had their work, but the women got bored.

"Zis week has been like a Carnival for us. Two ships in port at de same time. We never have that. But tomorrow they all leave. Once again Basseterre will be a quiet little town."

"The Cargo ship boys are staying another day," said Flabian.

"Oh. I did not know. Is dere any special reason zat de captain delays his departure?"

"If there is I don't know it," lied the young man.

"And you Mr Flabian, when are you leaving?"

"With the cargo ship boys," he replied. "They're taking me as far south as Trinidad. I thought a little time at sea would be good experience for my writing."

"Ah, how nice it must be to be an auter."

Pearl slipped her arm through his. "I do not trouble you?"

"Not at all," he replied awkwardly.

They drove a little way in silence. Pearl has her eyes glued to the windscreen. Twice she had made him turn back for she thought they had missed the turning. It was very quiet. There were a few shacks around, but no people: nobody to ask the way. Eventually, however, they found the turning and from there it was only a few minutes to the Black Rocks. To the writer they were a disappointment. The Black Rocks were simply black rocks and when he had photographed them they ceased to be of any interest to him. Pearl appeared not to be interested in the Black Rocks either. She was lying on the grass with one leg seductively displayed and propped up on an elbow.

"Come and photograf me," she said.

He took about ten snaps of her and then she said it was hot and she wanted a cool drink.

"We can stop off and have one," he suggested.

"No. Let's go back to my place and I'll prepare you a lovely fresh Planter's Punch. I make dem very well."

"OK. You're the guide."

On the way back Pearl spoke more about herself. She said she had been out of Cuba for just over two years. Both her parents had been killed in the revolution. Many of her friends were dead and no doubt she would have been too if she hadn't been fortunate enough to meet Jack. Jack, she explained, was her husband. He was much older than her and at the time was vacationing in Havana. He fell in love with her and as she quite liked him she accepted his proposal of marriage. She admitted rather coyly that she hadn't really loved him, but she wanted to get out of the country. Now, in St Kitts she led an entirely different life. It was a quiet life. She saw friends and friends saw her. At first she had spent a good deal of time learning English. She knew a little before, but it was by no means good enough for an English colony. Only now was she beginning to enjoy some of the easier English novels.

"Anyway, if I want to read at all it has to be in English. In a village like Basseterre Spanish books are quite unobtainable."

"Your English is very good. I wish I could speak Spanish half as well as you do English."

She smiled. "You are very kind." And then told him to turn left. "De house is on de corner. De sun is very hot now. Put de car in the garage or we shall cook on the way to Brimstone Hill."

They went in the house. After outside it was delightfully cool. The Venetian blinds were down and the stone floor no doubt helped to keep the temperature lower. She opened a couple of windows at each end of the house and this produced a pleasant draught. The lounge was spacious with a large sofa covered in a silky white fabric. There were a couple of easy chairs, a rocking chair and several pots with plants, both on side tables and on the floor. No doubt the greenery made the room feel even cooler. She invited him to make himself comfortable and went to prepare the drinks and soon she returned holding a large tumbler of Planter's Punch.

"That looks lovely," he said.

"You mustn't say that until you have tasted it."

He had a sip.

"Perfect. It's deliciously refreshing."

For a while they sat in silence. It was not an awkward silence, but one where two people were at ease without talking. They sipped lazily at their drinks.

Pearl broke the silence: "Do you like music?" she asked.

"Very much," he replied.

Flabian loved music. One of the snags of traveling in outlandish places is that there is very little opportunity to hear good music. Outside the big cities there are few orchestras and when you are constantly on the move as Flabian was you rarely got to know people well enough to ask them if you can listen to their records. He felt a thrill of excitement as he waited for her to ask him what he liked.

"Can you cha-cha?" she asked.

Flabian was a little taken aback. He liked dance music, but it wasn't what he expected. "A little," he replied.

"Good. I love cha-chas, but I cannot find anybody in St Kitts to dance with me."

The music started and they began to bounce about the floor. Then things began to happen fast. The Cha-Cha became a fox trot, then a slow and very soon they were tangoing cheek to cheek. Flabian felt drowsily happy. He liked Pearl's soft cheek against his and it gave him a pleasant thrill to hold her close. He could have gone on dancing in this intimate manner the whole evening, but suddenly he stopped and did something which he would never have dared do in a more sober frame of mind. He put his arms round Pearl's neck and then, as though it was the most natural thing in the world, kissed her full on the lips. Her lips were soft and warm and she did not resist, but returned the kiss. It was an embrace of two young people in the prime of life.

It was a little after 6:00 when Flabian left Pearl. She had shown him some photographs of Brimstone Hill and had told him should anybody ask where he had been that afternoon he was to say that he had seen the castle there. It took about an hour to the top of the hill and that would account for the way he had spent his time. They kissed goodbye and made arrangements to see each other the following evening.

Flabian felt as though he was walking on air as he made his way back to the hotel. Here were Perez and the skipper both quite convinced that they would be spending Monday night with Pearl, plotting against each other, even delaying their departure for an idle hope that neither would realize.

This reflection was followed by a stream of less pleasant thoughts. Suppose they found out? They might kill him, just dump him overboard. Who would know? Who would care? It struck him it would be unwise to travel with them. Then supposing both the skipper and Perez claimed they had spent Monday night with Pearl? How could he protest without giving himself away? It was all very awkward. He still wanted to travel with them; he'd promised; he really thought the experience would be good for his work. When would he get another opportunity like this? Then it struck him he could play safe: he had no obligation to see Pearl. If he told her he couldn't make it he'd have nothing to fear from Perez or the skipper. But he wanted to see Pearl again too. Constantly on the move like he was made meeting women difficult. There was never any time to develop a relationship. He felt he was perhaps like a sailor after all. There were women in every port. Maybe the skipper was right to make the best of them? Then he began to think that he was exaggerating the dangers. There was no reason to assume that the boys on the ship would ever learn about his affair. He might just be lucky. But he continued to dwell on the risks and remained in a state of indecision all day. Just before dinner, however, something happened and the whole burden of responsibility was lifted from him, for now fate took its hand.

Tuesday morning arrived. Flabian was going with the cargo ship boys after all. What had decided the thing for him was a phone call from Pearl. She was very sorry and all that, but she'd had a frightful headache all day and she felt if she didn't have an early night she would die. She hoped he would understand and "hasta luego" for the time being, it had been nice knowing him. Of course Flabian was not fooled: a headache my foot! It was far more probable that she'd had time to think things over and come to the conclusion that one indiscretion didn't mean she had to repeat it. It struck Flabian that a spontaneous act of unfaithfulness was perhaps excusable, but a premeditated one certainly was not. He had been lucky once. It was foolish to imagine more. Perhaps things had turned out all for the best after all. He had been told to be on board by 9:30 and they would sail about an hour later. It was now nearly 11:00 and he was on deck with Jardine and Moore. They were hanging over the railings searching the wharf for some sign of Perez and Thomas. Neither the second mate nor chief engineer had seen them the evening before and they had left no word about where they would be.

"You say they aint at the Palms ?" said Jardine.

Flabian shook his head. " I should have seen them if they had been."

"And what abart them bars on the wharf? Did ya manage to get a look in them?"

"No. I was thinking about other things."

"The bars are shut now," said Moore. "The only places they'll get a drink at this hour are at The Palms or The Royal."

"They're probably with some bloody whore," said Jardine.

"Perhaps they're trying to kid us they're with that damn Pearl woman," suggested the engineer.

"They can't both be with her," said Flabian.

"Yeah. But if they're not together they may be trying to pull a fast one over us."

"You mean they'll come back and tell us they've spent the night with Pearl?" said the writer.

"Yeah. Sure," replied the engineer. "Why not? It's not only their dough that's at stake, but their masculinity."

"It's going to be difficult to judge them," said Flabian.

Moore shrugged. "Most men are liars when they comes to talk about women. We'll be pretty safe if we assume they have both lost their bets. Still, I suppose we have to keep an open mind."

Jardine then said that he thought he could see a boat pulling away from the wharf. Moore looked through his binoculars. "It's Edmond," he said.

"Where the hell 'ave you been ?"yelled Jardine as soon as Perez was within earshot.

"Having one hell of time,"cried the other, but said no more until he had boarded. He looked tired and dirty, but gave the impression of being high. He said, in words usually not printed, what he'd been up to. In short he had had a wonderful time. He'd spent the night with Pearl and had only just got away.

"And where's George?" asked Moore.

Perez cocked his head upwards with a look of surprise. "Ain't he here?"

" We haven't seen him since yesterday lunch time," replied Moore.

"Where could he be?" asked Perez.

The others made a few suggestions. He was with a whore. He was too drunk to find his way back. He'd got mixed up with the time. Perhaps he had had an accident?

More smiled. "Nothing ever happens to George. The devil protects him. Satan couldn't afford to lose such a staunch supporter. Give him a little more time and he'll turn up."

They lingered on the deck, their eyes glued to the wharf. Now and again one of them speculated what had happened. At 12:30 they went down to lunch and it was during the meal that the skipper made his appearance. He staggered in on them in his usual state of stupor.

"Sorry I'm a few minutes late fellows. I've been 'aving a bit of fun in town."

"Where the hell have you been?" demanded Jardine.

The captain raised himself to his full 5' 6" . "'ere, that's no way to talks to your captain. It's my business where the 'ell I've been." Then added, as though it was the most natural thing in the world: "As a matter of fact I've been with Perla."

Moore shot Flabian a quick knowing look. "That makes two of you," he said.

"What d'ya mean it makes two of us?" cried the captain angrily.

The others told him what Perez had said.

The skipper became very red. He looked at Perez as though he was going to strike him. "He's a bloody liar. He wasn't with Perla. I was."

"Like hell you was," cried Perez. "You don't even know where she lives."

Thomas gave a forced laugh. "I can't tell you where she lives! I can tell you what the lounge looks like: stone floor, plenty of plants around, white silky sofa, green curtains, where the bedroom is and what the 'ell she was wearing."

Edmond looked stunned. "I don't believe you. You're lying."

The skipper was about to elaborate on his description when Moore cut him short. "You mustn't say anything in front of Edmond. We'll hear what you have to say separately."

"That's OK with me," said the captain. "I'll tell you whatever you wants to know. And if you don't believe me I'll 'old the bloody ship up another day and we'll go and ask Pearl."

After a brief pause Perez said a very strange thing: "Were you really with Pearl last night George?"

The others threw the first mate an odd look.

"Sure I was," replied the skipper. "'aint I just been telling you I was. I spent the whole damn night with her. I had a 'ell of a time slipping away because the damn maid arrived early."

Flabian was thinking fast. His thoughts were all over the place. The whole thing was incredible. He had a shrewd suspicion that some terrific con game was being played. But Thomas had described the house, the lounge, the arrangement of the rooms perfectly. He would wait and see what the first mate had to say. Then Perez came out with another piece of astonishing information:

"All right I admit I wasn't with Perla last night, but nobody in the world will be able to deny that I wasn't with her Saturday afternoon."

Flabian was so surprised that he jumped to his feet. "Good God, the woman is a bloody whore," he cried.

There was a deathly silence. They all looked at each other vacantly. A frown appeared on the skipper's head. He pressed his lips together, searched upwards as though he wanted inspiration, then he began laughing. At first it was a gentle laughter, but then his cheeks began to quiver, his belly began to roll, he groped for support on the table. His whole body began to shake. He held his sides. His face looked hideous. It was as though he was having some sort of epileptic fit.

"What are you laughing at?"cried Perez.

Thomas couldn't speak. He rocked and rocked.

Perez repeated the question more angrily.

It was no good. The skipper was splitting his side with laughter. He had no control. It was quite a time before he regained some sort of composure. The question was again repeated.

"That's precisely what she is," he got out at last. "I remember 'er quite distinctly now. She was in one of them high class brothels just off the Prado. She must have got out just before old Fidel Castro clamped down on all that business."

The others gasped.

"I think you'll be owing me four hundred bucks Edmond," said the skipper very quietly.

"Not so fast," said Moore. "She aint a whore now. She didn't take any money from you did she?"

The others admitted that she hadn't and Flabian knew she had taken nothing from him.

A long discussion ensued. When was a whore not a whore? Others could retire from their jobs, why couldn't she? Did it mean that because a woman was a whore once she remained one? Was it a life sentence? Was there no room for rehabilitation? Even when they were out at sea they continued to thrash the thing out. No conclusions were reached and eventually they decided to call all bets off.

The Colonial Secretary

"What an unhappy man," doctor Michael Grant repeated the words to himself again and again, for that was about the only impression that stuck with him after meeting the Colonial Secretary.

Grant, with quick little steps was returning to his guest house. He was a medium sized thickset man with a round jovial baby face, very black hair, somewhere in his late forties. As he walked along the dark road hugging its side, for there was no sidewalk he couldn't stop reminiscing about the evening. Yes, he had felt thoroughly uncomfortable the whole time. Even now he was still slightly tense.

When Grant arrived at the home of the Colonial Secretary just outside Bridgetown---in what appeared to be an upscale neighborhood, where the homes were large and varied with trim hedges and walls covered with poinsettia hiding most of the houses from the road—it was the Secretary himself who opened the front door. "Come in," he said. No smile, no handshake: he simply let Grant follow him into another room, large, with bay windows and high ceilings, clearly the sitting room. He was introduced to his wife Mrs. Hunt and a young man in his late teens or early twenties.

Hunt was probably in his early fifties, thin, tall, and with a firm handshake he appeared vigorous and healthy. His face was long with lined jowls and compressed lips, the eyes were distant as though people didn't interest him. His wife was slender with long auburn hair, a fair complexion, quite pretty thought the doctor, but what impressed him most was that she was a good deal younger than her husband. "Come round before dinner," she had instructed when he had phoned.

"Hugo is my son," said Mr Hunt and then asked Grant if he wanted a rum and coke.

"I'd love one."

Hunt left the room.

71

In and Around the Caribbean

Hugo was slouched in a wicker chair and had not risen when he gave the doctor a flabby handshake. He was very fair with a receding chin and sensual lips. He wore a t-shirt. He was certainly not Mrs Hutton's son, for she didn't look a day over thirty. Obviously the Colonial Secretary had remarried.

Grant sipped his drink. He asked his hosts how they came to be in Barbados. He enquired about the sites he should see. He tried to find out a little bit about the island. He asked many questions, but the replies were brief, though courteous and most of the time it was Mrs Hunt who did the talking. Hunt appeared to be preoccupied. He sat, drink in hand, staring vacantly in front of him. Hugo gawked at Grant and now and again twitched his nose and then scratched it. The doctor, in order to make conversation spoke a little about Trinidad and Brazil from where he had just come. He would, he said, be visiting some of the other Caribbean islands, ending his trip in The Bahamas and from there straight back to England.

The conversation was very one-sided. It made the doctor feel ill at ease. Hugo yawned once or twice. The Colonial Secretary had suggested that Grant go to the Tourist Information Office which would be in a much better position to answer his questions and no doubt would have documentation about the island. Grant was offered another drink. He was about to refuse but changed his mind when he realized he should stay a little longer otherwise they might think him rude. The Secretary served him and his wife another drink, but then excused himself and said he had some work to do. He apologized that his wife had not consulted him about the visit, for he would have suggested another day. Mrs Hunt apologized for not inviting him to dinner, but two of the servants were sick.

Time passed. There were brief bursts of conversation, none of particular interest to Grant or the hostess he felt. He got the impression that Mrs Hunt was just as eager to see him go as he was.

Eventually he looked at his watch and abruptly stood up. "Gracious me, I didn't realize the time. Dinner at the Guest House is served punctually at 7:00. The manageress is insistent about guests being on time."

All this was a lie, for dinner was served between 7:00 and 8:00. Besides, he could have quite easily skipped it if he had wanted.

The Hunts made no attempt to detain him and made no polite reference about having been pleased to meet him. As he stumbled across the Savannah the cool evening air smacked across his face and he felt invigorated as he wondered why the Hunts had seen him at all. They could quite easily have made an excuse about being tied up or something. After all he wasn't going to be on the island long. True, the person in Trinidad who had suggested he call them had claimed he was a good friend. Perhaps, in their official position, they viewed the invitation more like an obligation? A sort of way of publicizing the hospitality of the island. Soon the doctor reached the road and it was very dark and, though he was on the side he had to devote all his attention to not tripping-up on the jagged potholed tarmac. He was glad to have escaped the Hunts.

In the days that followed he tried to dismiss them from his mind, but somehow, like a recurrent dream, they persisted to haunt him. So obsessive became this preoccupation that one day he plucked up courage and asked the manageress at his guest house what she knew about them,

"Very little," she replied and then went on to say that politics didn't much interest her and all she knew about the Hunts was that he was Colonial Secretary; and from what she had heard, efficient, hardworking and respected in the colony.

"And what about his wife? Do you know anything about her?"

She shrugged. "Again only hearsay. I don't mix in those rarefied circles. I've been told she does her husband credit; that if it wasn't for her he wouldn't be where he is now. They say that if he's made Governor, and I hear there's a good chance he will be one day, it'll be thanks to her.

There was a pause and Grant saw his opportunity to put the question he'd been waiting for: "What was Mr. Hunt's first wife like?" he asked.

The manageress gave him a suspicious look. The doctor thought she was going to tell him to mind his own business, but she didn't and instead replied cordially: "I can't say I know much about her. It was a long time ago. A thing like that gets hushed up. I only know what everybody else knows: what I read in the paper." She looked down at the floor. "It was a very great tragedy...and she was so young too."

"What did she die of?"

The manageress fixed her stare on him. "She didn't die a natural death Dr. Grant. She committed suicide."

The doctor was half expecting such a reply. "What did she do that for?"

Again she shrugged. "Your guess is as good as mine. The papers didn't give many details. Highly strung I think they said."

"Wasn't there an enquiry?"

"Oh yes. The verdict was suicide. Cause unestablished."

"Is that all?"

She nodded. "Some people said he wanted to leave her. She was madly in love with him you know. But of course it was all rumor. There was no proof of anything."

Grant let the matter drop. He thanked her for answering his questions and began to wonder if Hunt's manner had anything to do with the mysterious death of his first wife.

A few days later, however, he left Barbados and continued his holiday journeying north. He saw the Colonial Secretary only once after that first meeting. It was on Broad Street and Hunt couldn't have missed him for they nearly bumped into each other. Grant had been about to say something, but the Colonial Secretary had appeared not to recognize him, for he ignored him completely and walked on. Grant was glad to be leaving Barbados. At first Hunt's manner rankled with him. The doctor knew that as far as the Colonial Secretary was concerned he was a person of no import but he felt that was no reason for him to treat him as he had done. After all he was a tourist and Barbados was poor and needed tourists. If the Colonial Secretary was an example of Bajan hospitality that was no recommendation for the island.

Grant malevolently decided that he wouldn't tell anybody to holiday there.

As Grant island hopped north Barbados and the Hunts faded from his memory. There had been so much that was new to see that his mind overflowed with fresh impressions. He had been enjoying himself and like so often is the case when you are having a good time you forget, or minimize, the unpleasant incidents that have befallen you. It wasn't until he was on the plane from Miami to Nassau that he was once again reminded of Barbados and the Hunts. Next to him was a man called Arthur Thompson. He was tall and slender with a long thin nose, tight lips and a dark complexion as though heavily sun tanned. He was a white Bahamian I learnt later. His eyes were a friendly brown and now and again they twinkled merrily as though laughing at some private joke. He was the editor of the leading local newspaper. He had been vacationing in the States and was now returning to work. His age was between forty-five and fifty. During the flight the two men got chatting. Grant told the editor where he had been and some of his impressions of the islands. Thompson then said something about New York and warned the young doctor to be prepared for the most outrageous prices in Nassau.

"Is it anything like St. Thomas?" asked Grant. "There the necessities cost the earth, but the luxuries are quite cheap. You can buy a damn good camera for as little as $80."

Thompson smiled faintly. "The only thing that's cheap in Nassau is liquor. If you want to get drunk it won't cost you much as long as you do it in private and don't get yourself up before the Magistrate."

Grant gave a little laugh and asked his neighbor if he could recommend a guest house. There was a pause and then Thompson suggested that the doctor put up at his place. "My wife's staying in New York until the end of the week. You can sleep in her room. I could easily get the maid to fix it up for you and it'll save you a bundle."

"That's very good of you," replied Grant somewhat awkwardly; "but really I don't want to put you to any trouble."

"No trouble at all. When my wife returns, if you still want to stay in Nassau, you can go to a hotel."

The doctor did not need much persuading and he agreed, profuse with his thanks to stay with Thompson until his wife returned .

It was after dinner that same evening, while they were sipping coffee, that the subject of Hunt came up."By the way," his host suddenly shot out: "did you meet a fellow called Charles Hunt when you were in Barbados? I think he's the Colonial Secretary there."

"In fact I did," Grant replied a little surprised to hear the name again.

"What did you think of him?"

"I only met him once," the doctor lied. "That was hardly sufficient time to get to know him."

Pause.

"I used to know him pretty well at one time," continued Thompson. "That was some years after the war. He wasn't married then. I was in Barbados at the time working for the local newspaper. The circumstances under which we met were rather unusual." He hesitated and gave Grant a quick look, as though he wanted to make sure he was listening.

The doctor did not reply and Thompson went on: "I had just arrived in Barbados and was looking for somewhere to live. I had been given an address by the girl at the Tourist Office and I went along to the place she suggested. When I rang the bell Hunt opened the door to me. He was a friendly fellow, well spoken and with a high intelligent forehead. He was just out from England, but wanted to move into a better flat as he found his present one too small. He invited me in and made me some coffee. 'I'll tell my landlady you want to move in when I leave,' he said. I gave him my phone number and he promised to pass it on to her.'

Thompson pushed a packet of cigarettes over to the doctor and asked him if he would like a liqueur.

"No thank you, but tell me a little more about Hunt. He seemed rather an interesting character."

The other lit himself a cigarette and went on: "Well I didn't think that chance meeting would develop into such a friendship. That very same evening he called me. 'Are you doing anything tonight,' he asks. 'No,' I replied.'Well, how about coming to a dance with a couple of teachers from the High School?'

"I was delighted and gladly accepted.

"Within the hour he had picked me up and we were on our way to the teachers' home to collect the girls.

"I was introduced to Anne and Joan. They offered us drinks and we got chatting. I took an immediate liking to Joan. She was slightly shorter than me, with very black hair and watery brown eyes. Her skin was a light coffee color and, although her features were quite European, there was no mistaking her color. She was rather more than a quarter caste, but nevertheless, I thought, extremely pretty. Her manner was gentle and feminine and she preferred to listen rather than do much talking . She was Bajan. Her father was English, but she never knew him. Anne on the other hand was quite different. She was Canadian. I don't know about her background, but she trained in England and was in Barbados on a three year contract. She was on the plump side, anything but attractive, but nevertheless pleasant and full of fun."

"There were four girls sharing the flat, but on that first occasion I only met Joan and Anne." He took a puff at his cigarette and for a moment watched the rings circle into the air. He went on: "Presently we went to a dance. It was a Saturday night and I remember there were several places we could have gone to. There was some discussion as to where we might go, but eventually we agreed to try them all. Charles had a car and there was no reason, if we didn't like one place, why we shouldn't move on to the next. That is exactly what we did."

"The evening was pleasant enough. We moved from dance to dance and I was pleased to get a glimpse of Barbados night life. Most of the time I found myself dancing with Anne. Every time I asked Joan for a dance she would give me the same answer: 'I'm sorry I've promised the next to Charles'. I noticed they danced cheek to cheek and that he held her tight. They seemed to get on capitally together and he looked gloriously happy and she was radiant. Everything was new to me and I suppose that I too enjoyed myself, though I didn't much like dragging Anne about the floor.

"Well, after that first evening Charles and I became institutions at the teachers' home. We were always there, or at least we were there as often as our respective jobs allowed. Charles was the only one of us who worked regular hours. The girls were often busy with extra-curriculum activities and sometimes spent their evenings correcting papers. As for me I never knew when my time was my own. In theory I only had two late nights a week. In practice it was often three or four.

"The only person I saw regularly was Charles. When I wasn't working at night I had dinner with him and if I was off during the day we lunched together. To cut a long story short we became good friends.

"Charles said he was pleased to be in Barbados. He had been a minor official in West Africa and had hated it there. The weather had been dreadful and a good deal of the time he had been ill. But worse than that was the fact that there had been no women where he was stationed. Now and again he had gone into one of the bigger towns for a weekend, but even there, he said, there was about as much chance of seeing a pretty woman in the street, as of seeing snow on the ground.

"'It gets pretty frustrating not seeing a woman for a couple of years,' he said. 'You begin, after a while, to think that anything in a skirt is desirable. This place as far as I'm concerned is heaven from that point of view.'"

I chuckled, but said nothing. I knew he was referring to white women. I couldn't imagine there being any shortage of black ones in West Africa. Of course, Barbados has an indigenous white population and there were always women who came out from England on various contracts, like some of the teachers for instance Then there were tourists. Of course by no means as many then as now.

"But let me get back to Charles. At the time he was what I would call a thoroughly decent fellow. He was straightforward; there was no side to him, and you got the impression that he said what he thought. He was serious, but not without a sense of humor; although now and again, I must admit, I did find it difficult to tell whether he was joking or serious. He was well educated. He had been to Harrow and had then read PPE[1]. at Oxford, where he had got a good second and a hockey blue. He was everything that an eligible young bachelor should be, and there were

---

[1] Philosophy, Politics and Economics

many mothers who had their eye on him for their daughters. As far as I was concerned there was only one thing about him which I sensed was rather odd; and that I attributed to his solitary existence in West Africa. He was friendly, honest, forthright and all the rest of it, and yet somehow there was some part of him that you could not penetrate. It was as though his soul possessed a secret which, although he knew existed, he himself could not fathom. On one occasion I broached him on the matter, but he laughed and then made a crack about the English school system: "What do you expect when I've been to a Public School?' he said. 'A Public School puts you in a mold. It makes you into a type: the Public School type. When you're old enough to realize that, it's too late: your character has already been formed.'

"Charles often used to speak of Joan. He thought very highly of her. 'She's a wonderful girl.' he would say.'She's the nicest girl I've ever met,' and then he would talk endlessly about all the qualities he thought she possessed:

"'She's intelligent too. She's worked herself up from nothing. It's not easy for a girl like her to go away and get a training in England. She must have been very good for the authorities to single her out.' He went on and on. No praise was too high for her.

"'Why don't you marry her?' I suggested half in jest.,

"'Hell man, that's exactly what I intend to do.'

"The next day Charles called me at work. He was very excited. He'd asked Joan to marry him and of course she'd accepted. He wanted to get married right away, before the end of the month if possible. Would I be best man? he asked.

"'I'd love to,' I replied. 'Shall I announce the engagement in the paper?'

"He hesitated and then said that he'd prefer to wait a while as he'd written to his parents as he wanted to put them in the picture. After all, he went on, he was their only son and it was only right that they should share his good fortune. He even went so far as to suggest that they might want to come out for the wedding.

"That evening I saw them both at the teachers' home. They were like a couple of love birds nestling in the corner on the sofa.

"There were three other teachers in the room including Anne, but as far as the two love birds were concerned, they were alone. I remember at the time I felt a kind of emptiness. I liked Joan, and although I'd never even taken her out I'd contemplated asking her to marry me. She was my type I felt, and in a way I was sorry that I was no longer in the running. I felt I had lost two good friends. I expect you know the feeling. When you're all single; you feel a common bond between you, so to speak: you're an equal amongst equals; but when your friends get married you become an outsider; you feel that they know something you don't and when you visit them it is no longer as an equal, but as a stranger. That, anyway, was how half of me felt seeing them snuggled up against each other so cosily. The other half of me, however, was pleased. I liked Joan and Charles and delighted in their joy and hoped they would be happy together. They were a handsome pair. They seemed to be well suited to each other and deserved all the happiness they could get.

"After their engagement I saw less of them. They only saw each other and had little time for me. Nevertheless, I still dropped in at the teachers' home now and again. Anne was always there to welcome me and keep me abreast of the latest news. Her tongue wagged furiously. She thought it absurd that they should be engaged: they had only known each other a month, and anyway they weren't, she thought, suited to one another. Charles, she described as an ambitious stuffed shirt, and Joan was very nice and all that, but...she shrugged, as though to say besides that there wasn't much else. The other teachers were more reserved with their opinions. They agreed that the whole thing had been a bit rushed, but both Charles and Joan were intelligent: they knew what they were doing; there was no reason why things shouldn't work out. They hoped they would anyway.

"Next time I saw Charles, I think it was about a week after he had broken the news of the engagement to me. He told me that the wedding had to be delayed: 'I think it'll be three or four months before we're able to get married,' he said, and then explained that Joan was on a yearly contract which, if she broke, would disqualify her from the bonus that was due her. He then said his own salary was only modest and they would need every penny they could get. It would be foolish to hurry things, he said. By the end of the year Joan would have her bonus and he would, in the meantime, living singly, be able to save.'That's what we've arranged anyhow. All being well we should be getting married just before Christmas.'

"He paused and I suggested that they could get married right away if they really wanted: 'After all there's no reason why Joan shouldn't carry on working even if she's married. It'll probably do her good and prevent her getting bored with herself.'

"Charles shook his head. 'No, I don't want that. No wife of mine is going to work. As soon as we get married she quits that school. I want her to get that sordid life out of her system.'

"'Have you told her that?'

"'Yes, we've discussed the matter and she agrees with me. She says she's sick of other peoples' children; she wants some of her own, and to spend her time pottering about the house.'

"I let the matter drop and we started talking about something else. After a while Charles left me. We arranged to meet Saturday. Joan was busy that day, but he'd promised to take Anne and one of the other teachers to the beach: would I come along too? I said I'd be delighted..

"The following morning Charles rang me up at 9:00 o'clock. He sounded very excited: 'Can I see you at once,' he said, it's very important'.

"'I'm in bed,' I replied. 'I was on late duty last night.'

"'I'm sorry if I woke you, but I must see you at once. Can I come round right away? I've taken the morning off. I rang the boss and said I wasn't feeling too well'

"I told him to come along if he didn't mind seeing me have breakfast in my pajamas.

"Ten minutes later he was with me. He thrust a letter in my hand. 'Read this,' he said.

"I read it. The letter was from his parents. They heartily disapproved of the marriage and would have nothing to do with it. Joan was obviously not the right girl for him: she had no background; she was a nobody, and they hadn't any prejudices against color and all that, but

81

lots of people had: what would everybody say when they saw him entering a room with a black woman? If he married such a girl his career would be at an end. And they'd held such high hopes for him, their only son. He'd done so well up to now: he'd distinguished himself at school and university; there was nothing to stop him; in time he would probably get to the top of his profession and there was no reason why he shouldn't even get a knighthood. Why spoil everything for a passing infatuation he'd almost certainly regret? Anyway they made it quite clear they'd be very disappointed if he married Joan.

"'What shall I do?' He searched me anxiously.

"I shrugged. 'That's not a very fair question? I can't decide your life for you.'

"'What would you do in my position?'

I hadn't the heart to give him the obvious reply: that I wasn't in his position. Instead I said I hoped that if such a situation arose my parents would be reasonable.

"He shook his head. 'My parents aren't like that. You don't know my father. He's very ambitious for me. He's seen his own aspirations crumble and he doesn't want that to happen to me.'

"'It's your life. You're old enough to know what you want to do with it. I'm sure your parents want your happiness. If you think Joan can bring you happiness then marry her.

"Charles threw me a defiant look. 'Hell man, you're right,' he cried. 'It's my life. I can do what I please with it. I've promised Joan I'm going to marry her and marry her I will.'

"His mood had changed completely. He seemed confident and in good spirits once again. 'Thanks Arthur, I won't forget what you've done for me'. He then went on to tell me what he'd nearly forgotten: `By the way I shan't be able to see you Saturday. My boss wants me to go to St. Lucia for a week. It's quite an important assignment and it'll give me a chance to impress the big boys. It's an opportunity I don't want to miss'.

"I congratulated him and then jokingly warned him not to be away too long otherwise I'd take his girl out.

"He laughed. Why don't you? I've promised to take her to the pictures Friday night: I'll be away then: I'm sure she'll be delighted to go

The Colonial Secretary

out with you.' He then added with a faint smile on his lips: 'Anyway even if she isn't I'm sure she'll enjoy the film; I'll tell her it's a good one.'

"'That's very kind of you,' I grinned.

"'Not at all'. His eyes twinkled and he got up to go. 'I'd be grateful if you'd publish that announcement of our engagement now,' he said and then left me.

"I took Joan to the pictures. I forget what the film was about, but I remember that while we were having a late snack she started talking. Charles had shown her the letter he'd received from his parents as he thought it wrong to hide anything from her. She'd have to know sooner or later what his parents thought and he preferred the truth came from him rather than anybody else. If they were going to be husband and wife they'd have to know all about each other; it was no use hiding things if after the wedding all their illusions were going to be shattered: no marriage could last on such slender foundations. Of course the letter had upset her, she said, but Charles was right: spouses had to be honest with each other. 'Naturally I gave him the option of withdrawing his offer to me'. A smile flickered across her face. `I don't think I'd have had the courage to if I hadn't known he'd refuse.'

"After a further hesitation she continued. She said that the letter had been a test for Charles: it proved that he could stand on his own two feet; that he was ready to defy his parents for her sake and in fact it showed that he really loved her. Now she felt sure of him, and she knew that when he said something he meant it. For her part she was certain she could make him happy."

"On that occasion I let Joan do most of the talking. She was full of Charles and spoke only of him, and it didn't require a genius to see that she was madly in love with him. I prayed that nothing should come between them, for I shuddered to think what might become of her should the marriage not come off."

Doctor Grant, the traveler in this story, had been silent for a very long time, and now he could not restrain himself from asking the obvious question: "And did it come off?" he asked.

Thompson waved the remark aside. "I'm coming to that," he said and then paused to light himself another cigarette. He went on: "Charles returned after his week in St. Lucia. Again he had to see me urgently. On his return to Barbados he had found another letter from his parents. In it they retracted all they said in the first one. If Charles thought he'd be happy with this girl they'd do nothing to oppose him; after all he was their only son and his happiness came before everything. If they'd been a bit outspoken in their first letter it was only the impetuosity of the moment. All parents wanted the best for their children: it wasn't that they'd had anything against Joan; it would have been the same for any girl; it was just that no woman was good enough for their son. But of course that was silly; on that basis he'd never get married and they did so want to see him settled. If he thought Joan was the right girl, they trusted his judgement. The marriage would have their blessing.

"'I'm so glad," I said when he'd finished reading the letter to me.

"Charles remained pensive for a while and then began to tell me that his week in St. Lucia had given him time to think. His parents were right. Joan wasn't the right girl for him. She had lots of faults and she was too old to correct them. She wasn't just eighteen and she'd be a millstone round his neck. He had his career to think of: it would be foolish to throw away his whole future just because of a passing infatuation. He didn't think he really loved Joan. It had been those two years in West Africa that had done it. He had been ready to fall in love with any woman who showed the slightest interest in him. It just happened to be Joan, but that did not mean she was the right girl. As far as his parents' recent communication was concerned, he dismissed it completely: 'My parents expressed their real feelings in their first letter. That was spontaneous. By the time they came to write the second one they'd had time to think things over. Their second letter was calculated: it was aimed at easing my feelings rather than theirs'. I know what my parents really think. It's all in black and white in that first letter.'

"He then went on to tell me that while he'd been in St. Lucia he'd gone to see a priest. The priest didn't know him so he obviously couldn't be biased.

"'And what did he say?' I asked.

"'He told me to break off the engagement,' continued Charles. 'He said that I obviously wasn't in love. Love was a whole hearted affair. I was undecided and it was impossible to be wholehearted and undecided at the same time.' The priest then went on to tell him that if he really wanted to marry Joan he should have taken the whole thing more slowly. Marriage was an important step in life and it shouldn't be trifled with; under no circumstances should it be rushed. Time would tell if he really loved Joan. If after a little while they really felt they couldn't live without each other then that was the time to start up a fresh romance. Such a romance would be based on more solid foundation. It could develop slowly and if they got married they would be sure that they were made for each other. Anyway, the priest told him that there was no harm in breaking off the present engagement.

"And is that what you propose to do?" I asked.

"Charles nodded. 'I think it's the best thing under the circumstances.'

"'You'll break Joan's heart,' I said.

'It's better that it should be that way now rather than later. The priest is right. I'm not ready for marriage.'

"'Are you sure it's the priest who has influenced you or is it that first letter that is still troubling you?'

"He threw me an angry glance. 'If I loved Joan I'd marry her.' His reply was a little curt.

"'Well there's nothing more to be said then." I paused and then as tactfully as I could suggested he sleep on his decision. 'Wait a week or so,' I said. 'Perhaps you'll come to a more balanced judgement then. Everything has been so rushed.'

"He shook his head. 'No. I've decided. I'm going to tell Joan right away. It's no use pretending something I don't feel. The longer I put the thing off the worse it'll be in the end. I know I've been a heel, but it's better that she should discover that now rather than later. She's given me the option to retract my offer and I'm going to take it.

"I begged him not to be in such a hurry. I wanted to delay any further rash action. I knew what this would mean to Joan and I hoped a little time would again change Charles' mind. I wasn't sure, you see, that he still didn't really love her. 'After all,' I said, `you were madly in love with the girl ten days ago. Your feelings can't have changed in so short a time. It's only natural you should be having cold feet. I've been best man before and I've seen grooms a few minutes before they have taken the vows. I know what you're feeling so don't think I don't. I know too that as soon as the ceremony is over you'll have forgotten all those qualms and be thinking only of the honeymoon. Of course I'm not suggesting that you should get married right away. What I am suggesting is that you think things over a little more. Don't be in too much of a hurry to break things off. See less of Joan for a little while or better still arrange to go away for a bit. When you return you'll know your own mind better and you'll be able to say for certain whether you want to marry her or not. I've a shrewd suspicion that you're all mixed up; that you don' t really know what you feel.'

"Charles gave a firm little shake of the head. 'No Arthur; I know exactly what I feel. I've been a heel long enough. I don't want to cause Joan any more suffering: it's better that she should know the truth right away.'

"I shrugged. There was nothing I could do. I'd done my best. Charles had always been impulsive and it would have been too much to expect to change his mind with a short pep talk. When he left he asked me to put another announcement in the paper to the effect that the engagement was off."

Thompson paused and asked his guest if he would have another drink. "'A drink can wait,' the doctor replied. 'I want know what happened next. Did Charles tell her?"

The host nodded: "He did."

"I think I can I can guess the rest," smiled Grant with a little air of confidence. Then, when Thompson kept silent, he went on: "Joan had a nervous breakdown. She was very ill, on the point of death and she perhaps even attempted suicide. The doctors said there was only one thing that could save her".

Grant paused and in vain searched Thompson's face for some sign of approval, an indication that would tell him he was on the right track.

His host remained impassive as though he was being questioned by a customs official. Grant continued: "Well, Charles took compassion on her. He did the only decent thing a man with his upbringing could do. He retracted all he said and promised to marry her."

Again the doctor hesitated and tried to divine what was going on behind that poker face, but Thompson said nothing. Grant went on: "Charles' promise did the trick all right. Joan got better and in due course they got married and decided to have children right away. They probably believed that having children would strengthen the bond between them. Joan was happy and Charles, although not happy, was not bored. Being married was a new experience for him; people treated him differently; he fitted into society and now he had new problems to worry about, and he didn't have much time to wonder if he loved Joan or not.

"In time they had a son. His name was Hugo; and they looked upon this little boy as the savior to all their problems. Their son would bind them together and make good their unrequited love; he would provide them with a common bond of affection, and through this they would grow to understand and love each other. This is what they had hoped, but unfortunately things did not turn out like that. Hugo failed to strengthen the tie between them. Gradually Charles grew bored. The novelty of marriage and being a father wore off. He didn't really love Joan and she wasn't much use to him in his career. He began to tell himself he'd been foolish to marry her, and he began to toy with the idea of leaving her. Their relationship worsened. What was at one time only a thought began to materialize: he threatened to leave Joan. The threats grew more and more frequent. She was all on edge, for she still adored him and all the while he was getting more and more impatient to be rid of her. At last the crack-up came. She just couldn't stand the tension any longer. She did the only thing that was open to her. This time she made no mistake and did the job properly." The doctor stopped, and then throwing Thompson a triumphant look exclaimed: "That's how it was wasn't it?"

Silence.

Gradually Thompson's quiescent face broadened into a wide grin. "That's a very good story. It would make excellent material for a novel."

He paused. "Unfortunately or perhaps fortunately, it has nothing to do with Joan or Charles. You see it wasn't like that at all."

Grant almost stifled a sob, but his host went on:"Charles and Joan broke off their engagement. From my point of view this meant that I saw more of them both. Of course Joan was very cut up about the whole business. She just couldn't understand why things had happened as they had. 'I always vacillate, feel uncertain about this and that,' she sobbed, 'but this time I was so certain.' She went on an on. She kept telling me she was on the verge of a nervous breakdown; that she hated her work and couldn't endure it a moment longer. 'At the end of my day I feel like a lump of putty,' she would say. 'I just can't go on like this. I must go away for a long long rest.'

"The days slipped by and she still carried on. She had grown thinner and I was rather concerned for her health, but she had a good little constitution and seemed to be able to endure far more than either she or I imagined. She still loved Charles although she was too proud to show it. Now and again she saw him at a party and she would make a point of speaking to him, and they behaved as though they were good friends. They explained to me that it was useless avoiding each other: Barbados was only a small place and they'd inevitably keep bumping into each other. If they cold-shouldered one another they'd make both their lives miserable, something neither of them wanted. The policy they adopted was live and let live. And I think that in this they were perhaps wise, for no good ever comes from resentment.

"Charles took the whole thing differently. He said he was pleased he'd broken off the engagement. He liked his liberty and joined a few clubs. He became a regular figure at all the fashionable Bajan dances, and once again solicitous mothers cast their eyes upon him. His attitude was hail fellow-well-met and he associated indiscriminately with anybody and everybody. For the most part I thought he mixed with the wrong set. He used to make out he was having a whale of a time and wanted that sort of life to go on for ever. It was only now and again, in his off-guard moments that he would tell me he hated the life he led. He wanted a quiet life, to get married and devote himself to his wife and work. In the meantime he dashed from one party to the next and I got the impression that he was completely unstable. Mothers now began to fear lest their daughters should get attached to him. I began to see him as the perennial bachelor, the play-boy of Barbados. I couldn't for the life of me imagine him married;"

Thompson paused, lit himself perhaps the tenth cigarette that evening and went on: "Well I was wrong. One day he rang me up at the office. It was about a year after he'd broken off with Joan. 'Will you put an announcement in the paper,' he said. He then told me he was getting married. He'd found just the right girl. She was a peach, but not only was she very beautiful, monied and all the rest of it; she was, most important, white. In addition to this she was well connected and would be an asset in his career. I congratulated him and promised to put the announcement in the paper.

"In due course I met the girl. Her name was Daphne and she was very much like Charles had described her; but that was not what impressed me. What did strike me was that in character she seemed very much like Joan. She too was sensitive, gentle and preferred to listen rather than talk. The girls could have been twin sisters as far as their temperaments were concerned. There was little between them, I thought, that could not be explained in terms of background. You could see that Daphne had had a charmed existence; that she'd been spoilt as a child and unburdened by financial worries. You could also see that Joan had been toughened by the very lack of these things." He paused and then smiled. "It is ironic that this should have determined the two girls' destinies; that Joan's background proved in the end to be her strength, whereas Daphne's background, with all its advantages, only led to her downfall." Thompson threw his guest a quizzical look. "You see when it came to a showdown, Daphne couldn't take it."

The doctor gave a little gasp. "I see it all now," he exclaimed. "Daphne married Charles, but the marriage did not go well and he threatened to leave her. Daphne could not stand the thought of him leaving her and committed that dreadful crime."

Thompson nodded. "I think that just about sums it up."

Grant went on excitedly. "But that means that Joan is alive and kicking?" he cried.

"Oh yes." Thompson gave him his disarming smile. "As a matter of fact, she's my wife."

Grant gasped. He was too bewildered to say anything and his host went on: "When Charles got married Joan's love turned first to hate and then indifference. As long as he he'd been single she still cherished the hope that perhaps one day he would change his mind and marry her. His marriage, however, put an end to all that, and then little by little she began to see him in a different light. For the first time she became conscious of his faults: to begin with these were few, but gradually, as time passed, they increased. She started to wonder what she'd seen in the man; she asked herself how she had ever loved him. She grew bitter. Her love turned to hate, and then, ever so slowly, her hate turned to indifference. 'Charles means nothing to me,' she would say. 'If he's hungry, lying in the gutter drunk, in prison or wherever he may be, that is no business of mine. As far as I'm concerned he doesn't exist.' It was then that I began to exist. Joan started to see me not only as a friend, but also as a lover and suitor. A little while later I proposed to her. We left Barbados and shortly afterwards we got married in Nassau.

"I followed Charles's subsequent career with interest. He returned to England for a spell. Then he was posted somewhere else, I forget where. A couple of years later he was back in Barbados. He got married. I never met his second wife, but I'm told she's done him credit. She was the sort of woman he needed; she had energy and push, and when he got discouraged she egged him on. Anne always said that it wasn't a wife Charles needed, but a mother. Perhaps she was right? Anyway he's got where he wants now. I'm told he stands a good chance of being Governor one day. But for all that I don't know if he's happy; if he wouldn't have been better off if he'd married Joan. I wonder?"

There was a long pause. The doctor did not tell Thompson that he thought he could answer his question, but instead changed the subject. I think I'm ready for that drink now." he said.

The Mother-In-Law

Outside it was hot and sticky. An incessant din of traffic throbbed the air: honking cars, rattling buses, police and ambulance sirens, fire engine bells, traffic whistles and more. It all sounded like an exceptionally noisy carnival, but it was just an ordinary week day morning in the capital of Trinidad. Port of Spain is a colorful town and the melting pot of many peoples. Here, at 10:00 a.m., the streets throng with activity: business men in white suits hurriedly going who knows where; street vendors raucously advertising their wares; tourists in Bermuda shorts leisurely shop gazing; Blacks arguing or moving their bodies to Calypso rhythm. You might even see an Indian woman wearing a Sari and with a ring in her nose. And, of course there are the Chinese: some in traditional dress, but most in Western garb. This is the scene on a typical morning in Port of Spain. Inside the B.O.A.C. offices, however, a very different atmosphere prevailed. It was cool, the blinds were down, fans purred and people spoke softly. Besides the whisper-like conversation and a muffled racket from the street, the only thing you really heard was the clicking of typewriters. David Payton, his chin in his hands, elbows on the desk, was studying some papers.

The telephone gave a buzz.

"Yes."

"A Mr Frith would like to speak to you sir."

"Who is he? What does he want?"

"He says he's an old R.A.F.[1] friend of yours."

Payton frowned, then gave a little gasp. "Good God. Peter Frith. What the hell is he doing here? Put him through."

"Hello."

"Hello."

"David?"

"Peter. That's a voice out of the past. Where are you? What have

---

[1] Royal Air Force

you been doing? What's been happening to you all these years."

"Hell David. It's good to hear you. I thought you were still in Hong Kong. It's only by a stroke of luck that I found out you were here. Fellow I met in London gave me your address. But tell me about yourself. How are you?"

"Nothing to tell you old man I stopped flying nearly three years ago. Been in Trinidad ever since. A desk job. I don't lead a very exciting life. Work, the club, a little swimming; now and again I play some cricket. Still single. But how about yourself? What are you doing? Did you get to university as you hoped?"

Frith replied that he had, and suggested they meet.

"Sure. Whenever you like. How about this evening after I've finished work. We could meet at the Queen's Park Hotel. The bar is air-conditioned." And so it was arranged.

On the dot of 6:00 David Payton, tall, thin with black hair beginning to thin around the temples, pushed through the swing doors into the lounge-bar of the Queen's Park Hotel. He looked vacantly about him. A man rose from one of the tables and came towards him.

"Good God Pete. I hardly recognized you. What have you done to yourself? You're looking quite respectable."

"Thanks."

They shook hands and went and sat down.

Frith wore a white tropical suit. His build was similar to Payton's. He was probably about the same age, somewhere in his mid-thirties. He had emerald eyes, a long face with a sensual look around the lips. His smile was warm and friendly, like that of a schoolboy who had just been given a bar of chocolate. Both men had color in their cheeks and looked healthy. But what struck Payton most was the change in Frith's manner. He appeared poised and confident. Ten years before he had been awkward, slovenly and full of resentments.

Drinks were served. Then for the next fifteen minutes or so they brought each other up to date. Frith was an Agricultural Economist and was just beginning a three year contract with the Trinidadian Government. He had arrived two days before on the Hubert, a cargo ship. He had married well, a little over 18 months before. His wife's family had a long ancestry which could be traced back to the Tudors. Mary's father, before his sudden and premature death, was in the House of Lords. Mary would be joining him (Pete) in a couple of months. He wanted everything to be easy for her. He would find a house, get some servants, a car, join a club or two and hopefully make a few friends. He would put a few feelers out for Mary too. He wanted her to do something, otherwise she'd die of boredom. She was an intelligent girl and had a degree in English from London University. He thought a teaching job or working in the library might be a good idea. She had, apparently, experience in both

"I want to have everything ready, lined up, by the time Mary arrives." Frith continued. "She's always had things fairly easy and I don't want to be the one to change that. She wanted to come out with me, but her mother didn't want her to arrive in a strange place with nothing prepared. I didn't want a fuss or anything, so I said I'd blaze the trail so to speak." He paused and had a sip at his drink. "I'm beginning to regret my promise now. It's the first time Mary and I have been separated. I left England just over two weeks ago and already I'm missing her terribly. I'm counting the days to when she'll be here."

"What made you come to Trinidad?" Payton cut in.

Frith threw his hands in the air, as though fate had made the decision for him. "I don't really know. I think I wanted a change. The weather is good, the pay is better than in England." He hesitated and looked at his friend in the eyes, then went on: "I think I can speak to you honestly. Well, if you want to know the truth: the real reason why I came here was to get away from my mother-in-law. You don't know how lucky you are not to have one. Believe me, before you get married make sure you've got a decent one."

Payton laughed. "I'll remember that," and then added cheerfully: "Anyway, you'll be a long way from the old girl here."

Frith scowled. "Not for long. She's coming out for a visit at the end of January."

David Payton, who was not taking Frith too seriously, smothered a giggle.

The other went on: "It wasn't doing us any good with Lady Shackleton on top of us all the time. I was going mad. Do you realize that not a day passed without Mary seeing her mother. As for the telephone calls I dread to think how many there were. Fortunately I was at work most of the day and didn't know what was happening. Mary is quite capable of doing things for herself, but her mother seems to think that she should be like some sort of Victorian woman whose chief virtue was her inability to do anything for herself. That may have been fashionable 80 years ago, but it isn't now. Mary plays the piano and is well read. She's worked around books and schools, but her mother didn't like that and now she's working for some charitable organization. Do you realize that before we got married she didn't know how to darn a pair of socks, or boil an egg for that matter? I don't think she'd done a day's housework in her life. Mary admits that she is over-influenced by her mother, but says she can't help herself. She thinks that coming out here will change things. Lady Shackleton believes that her daughter should perfect herself in the social graces and delicate accomplishments, so that one day she would attract a rich and Lordly husband. Instead she got me, who left school at sixteen and the son of a Liverpool hairdresser."

He paused, took a large swill at his drink and asked Payton if he was boring him.

"Hell no. Go on. I'm quite content to listen."

Frith needed no encouragement. Two weeks on board a ship with mostly Portuguese and Blacks had given him small opportunity to talk about himself. Now he was only too pleased to have a sympathetic ear.

"I'll start from the beginning. As you know before I joined the forces I was a hairdresser. When I came out it seemed that there wasn't much else for me to do, so I went back to my old job. After the RAF it wasn't easy. Everything seemed so narrow and petty and I could see that my prospects were poor. Hell, I didn't want to be like my old man. I resolved to try and go to university. It wasn't easy for me. I had a good School Certificate, but that wasn't enough. I registered for some extra-curriculum studies and for the following two years worked my ass off. Anyway, to cut a long story short, I got a County Scholarship to University College. The rest, after those two hard years of almost private study, was comparatively easy. I got a good second class degree."

Payton nodded approval and said that Frith had done well for himself. "You always said you'd get a degree."

Frith waved the remark aside. He had begun his story and didn't want any interruptions. He continued: "It's strange in a way that I should have fallen for Mary. She was really quite opposite to me. I was in a rut because I was poor and my parents laughed at me when I read a book or tried to improve myself. She, until she married me, was in a rut because she was rich and had everything too easy. Of course she was well aware of her circumstances. She was awkward and shy, and in the presence of her mother always felt like a child. She has told me countless times that it's very difficult to make an effort when you don't have to. I met her at Senate House. I used to see her in the library and now and again in the refectory. She was always on her own and this aroused my curiosity, for I thought her quite attractive. One day I plucked up courage and joined her table. We got chatting. At first I felt ill at ease, for I instinctively knew we were on different sides of the fence. Anyway, I invited her out a few times. Then she suddenly left her job. Her mother had arranged for her to work with this charity. Of course, now I know that Lady Shackleton probably suspected that her daughter was seeing somebody (not the right somebody) and wanted to put a stop to it. Anyway, though it was more difficult, I did continue to see Mary and soon we realized that we were madly in love. I asked her to marry me. She accepted, but said it wouldn't do to get married right away as I had no money or position. I had just got my degree and we agreed that there was no harm in waiting a while. That would give me time to establish myself in a decent job. Mary's family knew nothing about me. At first I was a little surprised that I had never been invited to her home, but then she explained that her mother wasn't too well and would probably be against the marriage. It was important, she thought, to broach her mother at an opportune moment.

"In due course I got a job at the Ministry of Agriculture. I thought the time ripe to get married and told Mary this. She hedged and suggested we wait a little longer. I said there was no point: even if we didn't get married right away we could at least announce the engagement. I told her I would go and see her mother the following day. Mary tried to put me off, but when I started questioning her about her love for me gave way, though she did again warn me about her mother being a difficult woman—of the old school and all that. I waived her remarks aside and said I felt sure her mother would like me. Little did I know what was in store for me."

"Next day I did go and see Lady Shackleton. Mary had spoken to her about me and the dear woman was all ready to receive me. She did so with the utmost civility. She couldn't have been more correct. Her manner was such that I imagined she used when interviewing a prospective butler. She was stiff, cold and extremely informal. I got the impression she didn't really want to see me at all and had done so only for Mary's sake. She explained that I wasn't quite the person she had in mind for her daughter; that Mary had only been used to the best and though I would no doubt try and give her that I couldn't do what was beyond my means. She felt sure I loved Mary dearly; she didn't want to be cynical, but sometimes the most perfect love matches ended up on the rocks for sordid material reasons. Of course, she went on, it would be possible to settle a handsome dowry on Mary, but she was certain that I wasn't the sort of man who wanted to live off his wife's money. She went on and on. Her tongue was devastating. There was nothing she missed out that might stop the match. She said that Mary was sensitive, still a child with no real knowledge of life. At her age she couldn't possibly know her own mind. She was heir to a great fortune and with no father, she (Lady Shackleton) had a great responsibility for her only child. She said much more, but I can't remember. At the end of an hour and a half she informed me that the interview was at an end and she would be grateful if I didn't see her daughter any more. She added that she knew she wasn't being fair to me, but thought it right to be honest and tell me straight what she thought. I was shown the door. I left like a lamb. I was speechless. It was as though I had been hit by a stroke."

"By next day, however, I had regained my composure. I loved Mary and knew she loved me. I determined that I would let nothing stand in our way. I had arranged the day before to meet Mary at Harrods for tea after work. As I went up the escalators I had some qualms about whether she'd be there, for I had little doubt that her mother would have given her strict instructions not to see me. I needn't have worried: she was there before me. She looked pale and sullen, and I knew, before even telling her of the events of the previous evening, she was aware of them. We discussed the matter at length. Eventually I said that I would go and see her mother again. Mary shook her head and said it would do no good. I was adamant and told her I couldn't see any harm in trying."

There was a pause while we ordered more sandwiches.

"Well, nobody can say I didn't try. I don't know what I didn't do to get hold of Lady Shackleton. I phoned. I went round to the house and each time the maid informed me that she had been given instructions not to receive me. I begged her; I tried to bribe her; once I even tried to force my way in. Politely she informed me she would call the police. There was nothing I could do and I told Mary the initiative must come from her. `What do you want me to do?' she asked. I had given the matter a good deal of thought and told her she must tell her mother we would elope." (Frith chuckled). "Mary was horrified. She thought I was out of my mind. The idea, she exclaimed, was monstrous and she didn't know how I could even think of it. She said it would tarnish the family name, that it would kill her mother, that she would feel uncomfortable without her mother's blessings. She went on and on. I had no arguments against her, except one: did she love me? If she did, no reasons would be sufficient to stand in our way. If she didn't, the flimsiest excuse would adequate. I had her and she knew it. It took her nearly three weeks to come to a decision."

Payton got up to go to the toilet. When he returned Frith went on as though there had been no interruption: "Well, the whole thing worked like a charm. Lady Shakteton didn't die on the spot. On the contrary she sent for me immediately. She told me I was lower class and a rotter, but she had the family name to think of. Then she bluntly asked me how much I wanted. At first I didn't know what she was talking about, but then she made herself abundantly clear. To begin with I was shocked, then I began laughing. I told her all the money in the world would not be enough to pay me off. I loved her daughter and wanted to marry her. Lady Shackleton was quiet for a very long time. I was nervous I must admit. I imagined she might be conjuring up some ghastly plot. It struck me she might employ some thug to dump me in the Thames. Less extreme she might get me fired from my job, any job. No doubt she had influence. I felt like quietly sneaking out of the room without a murmur. But I needn't have worried: Lady Shackleton was thinking along entirely different lines. She suddenly announced her decision. She didn't approve, but nevertheless divorces were easy to get nowadays and she'd let Mary see for herself what I was really like. The whole thing was an anti-climax."

"We got married. Lady Shackleton insisted on a huge wedding. It was a gigantic affair and I felt ill at ease amongst all those Lords and Ladies. I was pleased when I found a flat of our own and we began to settle down. I didn't have much money and I wasn't going to use Mary's.

The place we got was small, clean, comfortable. No luxuries. Mary liked it and so did I. Of course we had no servants. Mary was becoming domesticated and she was quite enjoying it. We would have been perfectly happy if it hadn't been for Lady Shackleton. She was always there and had a knack of putting us ill at ease. She'd remind us about how small the flat was; she noticed that Mary's hands were getting hard; she brought us food as though we were short. If we said anything she would smile engagingly and say she was only trying to help. Heat, rain or fog she always came round. Nothing deterred her. When we said we might go to the Lake District for a holiday she said it was an excellent idea: she hadn't been there for years; she would join us. When I complained to Mary she said she could hardly tell her mother she wasn't wanted. I asked 'why not?'. But she replied she felt guilty enough marrying me against her mother's will. She didn't want to make things worse. Lady Shackleton played her cards admirably. She never said anything directly. It was always the innuendo, the disapproving look, or the indifferent do-as-you-like attitude. Her power over her daughter was immense. Naturally Mary didn't quite see things the way I did. She said her mother was a poor lonely sick woman, very attached to her daughter, who couldn't believe that she was now grown up and had a life of her own. 'She's doing her best for me,' she said. I told Mary she was talking rubbish. Her mother had the health of an ox. She was quite determined to break up the marriage. She planned everything with the skill, cunning and craftiness of Catherine de Medici.

"And you know how Mary reacted to that? I thought I had gone a bit overboard. I was about to apologize, but she came up to me and gave me a motherly kiss on the forehead. 'I don't think you like mother,' she said. A few minutes later she had completely forgotten that I had compared her mother to one of the wickedest women in Europe.

"Things drifted on for about a year. I was slowly going crazy. I told Mary the only thing we could do was go abroad. I had no idea where. The further away from London the better, I thought. I didn't tell Mary this, but I started to go through the classifieds. When I saw that an Agriculture Economist was wanted in Trinidad I decided to apply. In due course I was accepted. I felt that distance and climate would be a sufficient deterrent to Lady Shackleton following us. I must say I felt better than I had for a long time. ." He shrugged. "My elation didn't last long. As I told you she'll be visiting at the end of January. My only hope is that she won't like the place and won't stay long. Well, that's about it: what I'm doing here; what's been happening to me these last few years."

"You make marriage sound pretty awful."

Frith smiled: "Mary's a wonderful girl. I didn't know how much she meant to me until I came here. Our marriage is the one thing I don't regret."

"But what about her mother? What are you going to do with her when she comes out?"

"Grin and bear it, I suppose. She can't stay forever. All her ties are in England, except of course for Mary."

"What happens if she likes it here?" said Payton.

The words acted as though Frith had been given an electric shock. "Damn it man whose side are you on? She's not going to like it here, and that's all there is to it. I'll do my bloody best to make things as uncomfortable for her as possible. She can go to hell. I'll make damn sure she doesn't like Trinidad.".

Payton kept a diplomatic silence.

A moment later Frith was calm and they ordered another round of drinks. They chatted a while longer. Payton offered to show him round the island. They left to have dinner together.

In the weeks that followed Payton and Frith saw a lot of each other. Frith had been busy making arrangements for the arrival of his wife. His decision to come early and before he was due to start work had given him ample time to make the most important preparations. He had rented a house, bought furniture, linen, kitchen utensils and other things he thought they might need. He had engaged some help, bought a car, obtained insurance and the various licences. He had joined the Public Library, a Country Club and had made enquires about other clubs. He had been so busy that he hadn't had much time to moan the absence of his wife. Gradually, however, as preparations began to wind down he found himself with more time. Payton took him to San Fernando, Maracas Bay, and a few other tourist highlights. He showed him the Botanical gardens, the Asphalt Lake, Trinidad's night life and introduced him to some of his friends. Notwithstanding these distractions, Frith was becoming increasingly restless and yearned for the arrival of his wife.

"I really miss her," he told Payton. "I don't know how I'm going to get through these next couple of weeks. I'm not much good at being celibate. Before you're married it's not so bad. Expectations are much lower, but the anticipation is always there. Every woman is an opportunity. I don't know how you manage. You ought to get married. It's a wonderful thing. Half your problems go overnight. I'm speaking from experience."

He'd then sing the praises of the marriage institution. Monogamy was natural to man. It wasn't fun having one woman after another. You got to know none and you could never quite be yourself and relax. He talked about their life in the RAF, their sordid love affairs and how he hated them and yet had persisted because there was nothing better. He'd go on and on and then quite suddenly he'd become sentimental and start talking about Mary again. His voice would change, his eyes would soften, even the very words he used seemed to mean something different. Payton knew, without even listening, that he was talking about his wife. Frith had shown photographs of her. She was slightly shorter than her husband, with dark hair, high cheek bones, a long nose. Her face was round and chubby and the close-ups revealed a few freckles. She looked a bit girlish Payton thought, as though still an adolescent. Her figure was good however, bulges in the right places, long legs, though not particularly tall. Frith didn't stop telling him what she'd done for him.

"She's given me self respect; made me feel confident, more of a man. Since I met her I haven't looked at another woman."

Payton said very little, but he did notice that his friend still had a roving eye. By the time Mary arrived he felt he knew all about her. They were both at the cay-side when the ship arrived. Frith was very agitated as he strained his eyes to single her out from the crowds on deck. Then he gave a cry of triumph. "There she is." And he began waiving frantically. He pointed her out to Payton. The boat was still not docked and all he could see was her yellow buttercup dress, the dark hair and chubby face.

A little later they were formally introduced. Payton felt seeing her in the flesh did not alter the impressions he had formed of her from the photographs. They, in fact, did her credit. Her cheeks appeared to have more color, her eyes seemed more lively. It struck him that she was perhaps tired after the trip. She had an exquisite accent and spoke confidently, though he sensed that underneath she was very shy and sensitive. She had, he thought, youth, sincerity, a certain charm, but was not pretty in any classical sense. That evening he called them to offer his help, but the number was always busy. No doubt the phone was off the hook. He decided to let Peter contact him.

During the weeks that followed David Payton saw little of the Friths. He did, however, notice a change in Peter. His eyes sparkled, he looked vital and he often laughed and joked. He told Payton that it was wonderful to have Mary to himself and be free of his mother-in-law. He could hardly believe his good fortune. It was like a second honeymoon. If only he could freeze time. He was supremely happy.

"You'll soon be off to England," he said to David one day when they met on the street. "You must come round for a drink before you go."

"I'd love to," was the reply.

"When exactly do you leave?" said Mary who was standing next to her husband. .

"All being well, round December 20th, but I can't give a precise date. It all depends when seats are available." He then explained that airline staffers only paid 10% of the normal fare, but had to wait for a seat.

"When you come round remind me to give you mother's phone number," said Mary.

"You can try and persuade the dear woman not to come out here. Tell her Trinidad is a dreadful place: it's dangerous and the weather's awful ."

"Darling, what will David think of mother if you say all those horrid things about her?"

Peter threw his wife a mischievous look. "David knows all about your dear mother darling. I wouldn't worry on that score."

"I'm afraid Peter isn't very fond of mother," Mary said .

Peter ignored his wife: "The first time you meet Lady Shackleton she'll be sweetness itself. You'll fall for her completely. You'll think she's quite the most charming woman you've ever met. She'll talk to you about this and that. She'll listen to you and offer you tea, hot scones and treacle. She'll captivate you like she does everybody else. But if you get to know her you'll discover she's selfish, mean, calculating..."

"Stop it Peter. It's my mother you're talking about. I won't have you speak about her so." She tugged his arm. "Come. We had better go before you say any more things you shouldn't."

Payton left for England within the week. He had Lady Shackleton's phone number and address with him and Mary had reminded him that her mother would be leaving for Trinidad on January 10.

It wasn't until after the new year that he met her. His first week in London had been hectic: buying presents, seeing friends, just walking and looking at the shops. Trinidad was very far away from his thoughts. As soon as he got in touch with Lady Shackleton she invited him round. Mary had told her he was coming. It was nice of him to look her up. He must be very busy. She would be delighted to meet him. Would he be able to make Sunday tea? Just the two of them. There would be nothing special and they could have a nice long chat. She was eager to learn about Trinidad and hear his views about the place. She was very worried about Mary and did so want reassuring. "Until Sunday," and she then hung up.

The house was in Avenue road. It was large, modern and newly painted. In the drive stood a Rolls Royce. Payton felt out of place as he rung the front door bell. A maid in a lounge. "Her Ladyship will be with you in a moment," she said. Payton looked nervously around. There were a couple of Turners on the wall. There was a cabinet with a snuff bottle collection in it. The carpets looked Turkish or Afghan, he didn't know the difference. He wondered what he would think of Lady Shackleton? No doubt Frith was exaggerating. Would she really be charming? Maybe her daughter's wedding wouldn't even be discussed. His thoughts were broken off when she entered the room.

"I'm so sorry to have kept you waiting." She smiled and gave him a dainty hand. "I'm so glad you could come. Mary's told me all about you."

Lady Shackleton had silver grey hair. She was tall and slender, with a long aristocratic nose, thin lips and blue-green eyes. She wore a dark green coat and skirt, which gave her the look of a business woman. There was an ornate diamond broach on her lapel and on her wrist an intricately woven sapphire and diamond bracelet. Payton thought her smart, elegant and aristocratic. She asked Payton about his trip, how he was enjoying London, did he like it in Trinidad? She asked a few questions about the place. She had never been and was looking forward to seeing it and, of course, Mary.

"I'm terribly worried about her, so far way, in a strange country and me not there to help. She's never been further than the Continent and Trinidad must be so different. They tell me it's very dangerous to go out at night, even for a man. I've heard such dreadful things about the place:

why only last week I was told a ghastly story of an Indian woman who chopped up her husband's three children because he left her out of his will."

Payton, then diplomatically told her things weren't as bad as all that. It was true that there were a lot of murders on the island, but most were family affairs and took place outside the city. It was really quite safe in Port of Spain if one kept to the main streets. "Anyway," he continued: "Mary's in good hands and when I left her was in excellent spirits.

Lady Shackleton shrugged and said she was perhaps worrying unduly, but the truth was she didn't trust Mary's husband. "I never approved of the marriage," she went on; "but nowadays young people are so independent: they think they know best and you can't tell them a thing. It's really so silly because it means that all their elders' experience is wasted. It's as though students were forbidden to learn from the past and had to discover everything from scratch for themselves." She threw up her hands as though resigned. "Well, I suppose it can't be helped. I only hope I'm with Mary when things go wrong. I'd never forgive myself if I was an Ocean away and she really needed me."

"Don't you think things will work out?" Payton asked a little hesitantly.

Lady Shackleton gave him a hard look. "I haven't the slightest doubt they won't. I'm afraid I don't believe in miracles. I've seen too much."She paused before going on. "I suppose you would like to know why I've been so opposed to the marriage all along?"

"I'm not very sure of the reasons I must admit."

At that moment the maid came in with a tray and he was offered tea, scones and cucumber sandwiches.

Lady Shackleton continued: "You are going to think me an impossible snob, but my views are quite conventional and as old as Adam. It's the old story of marrying outside one's class. It just doesn't work. Time and time again I have seen marriages end on the rocks because young things thought they were in love and that was all that mattered. It's difficult enough for two people to understand each other, but the gulf of class makes it that much harder. It's as though they didn't speak the same language. Take Peter and Mary for instance: besides believing they're in love they've absolutely nothing in common. Mary has had the best education money can buy: Peter was brought up in the slums of Liverpool. Mary's had the chance to listen to good talk and meet some of the finest people in the country: Peter, poor boy, probably had to associate with drunkenness, crime and no doubt the only talk he heard was smut.

"I know you're thinking all this is over and done with. Peter has moved up in the world and isn't like his father. Well, that's only partly true. As far as Peter's job is concerned he's done himself well. I'm the first to acknowledge it. But in another sense he's always remained the Liverpool street urchin. He's got no class, no distinction: you can see right away that he hasn't been to a Public School. I'm always dreadfully embarrassed when I have friends round and he's there. He simply doesn't fit in. Peter's at ease in a bar, watching a football match or listening to dirty jokes with the boys. I don't know how Mary could have fallen for him. They're simply poles apart.

"Then there's the question of money. I always say that money should marry money. That way you at least know that one spouse isn't marrying the other for his or her wealth. But even if that isn't the case money creates barriers. It's not so bad if the man has it. It's pretty near disastrous if it's the woman. For instance, Mary has seen so much more than Peter. He always feels embarrassed about it. That's why he's so keen on keeping her on what he earns. Of course she doesn't say anything, but it must be agony for her to cook, do the washing up, housework when she could be reading or playing the piano."

He was about to interrupt, to say that in Trinidad they could have all the servants they liked. She continued as though she hadn't noticed he wanted to say something: "It's not so bad for him: he's never had the little luxuries. But for Mary it is a real sacrifice. Of course, now she's young, they haven't been married long, it's all new and she perhaps enjoys the experience. But when she gets older I have little doubt she'll see and feel things differently. The novelty of drudgery will wear off and only its bitterness will remain."

She paused and offered him another sandwich.

"Well, there it is Mr Payton. You perhaps think I'm a foolish old woman crossing my bridges before I get to them. But believe me I've seen a lot and I can tell you that marriages outside ones class don't work."

"In Trinidad they'll have all the servants they want. In fact they've already got three."

"I don't think you quite understand me," said Lady Shackleton. "I know my Mary. She'll be homesick, so far away from home. She'll want to return. And what then?"

Payton, as politely as he could, said he thought that for the time being they were very happy.

"Ah," she sighed. "But for how long?"

"I hope it'll last to the end of their days."

Lady Shackleton threw him a piercing look. "I think there's a lot I know about Peter that you don't," she said.

He gave her a curious look but kept quiet.

"Before I met Peter formally I made it my business to get to know as much as possible about him. I was well aware that Mary was going out with somebody and it was my duty to find out who it was. I didn't say anything to her as I didn't want her to think I was prying. I hoped he was no more than a passing infatuation. It wasn't long before I realized it was more serious. I felt I had to put my foot down. When he came round to see me I didn't mince words: I told him that I didn't want a rake in the family."

When she saw her guest's bewildered look she hurriedly went on: "Yes, Mr Payton, a rake. I do not use the word lightly. I discovered more about Mr Frith than I had bargained for. I was well aware of his bouts of dissipation in the RAF." She shuddered. "It's horrid to think him with my Mary and with all those ghastly women. `Wild oats', and that's a polite way of putting it, may be natural in the working classes, but they're certainly not natural with the better type of person."

"Perhaps now you are beginning to understand why I was so opposed to the marriage. And it was something I couldn't mention to a soul. It was embarrassing; and I had to keep telling Mary he wasn't suitable. I could hardly give her the real reason."

Payton felt flushed. He wondered what she knew about him. He felt forced to say something: " That was a long time ago Lady Shackleton. Peter looks back on that period with horror. I'm sure it was just an unfortunate phase. It was all before his life had direction and he began to make a career for himself." He stopped abruptly, for he was conscious that Lady Shackleton was eyeing him with disapproval.

"Perhaps Mr Payton you are not aware that Mr Frith has been consorting with ladies of the street as recently as four months before his marriage."

"I didn't know that," Peter said feebly.

She continued: "There's no trusting that man when a woman is around. Why do you think I've been on top of them all the time?" The question was rhetorical. "It's not just that I want to be with Mary when he lets her down, but also because I exert a sobering influence on him. As long as I'm around he behaves himself. I wouldn't be at all surprised if getting a job in Trinidad was to get away from me. I'm told the women in Port of Spain are very beautiful."

The maid came in and cleared away the tea things.

Payton felt like saying that he was certain that, except for Mary, Peter wasn't interested in other women. He refrained however. After all he hadn't the slightest idea what Peter did with his spare time.

As soon as the maid was out of earshot Lady Shackleton continued: "And in a place like Trinidad where, I should think, morals are so low he wouldn't have any difficulty in doing what he pleases. Anyway,

I've at least had the good sense not to settle any money on him. The family's fortune will go to the children if they have any or, of course, Mary should they split up. It would have been ironic if in a few years he'd been living with another woman on the fruits of the Shackleton fortune." She again reiterated how worried she was about her daughter and only hoped she would be near her before anything dreadful happened.

"I'm sure everything will be all right," said Payton.

"I only hope you're right; but I can't help having my doubts. I can't wait to get to Mary."

They chatted a while longer and in due course Payton took his leave.

He did not get back to Trinidad until March and it wasn't until a few days later that he got in touch with the Friths. He spoke to Peter who seemed to be in a terrible state. Without a word about Payton's trip he asked if they could meet right away.

"What's happened?" asked Payton.

"I don't want to talk on the phone."

They arranged to meet in the bar of Queen's Park Hotel at 6:00. When they met Frith said he was too restless to sit down. "Let's walk about the Savannah. A little exercise will do us good."

"Fine."

As soon as they were away from the road Frith came straight to the point. "Thank God you're back Dave. I'm in a terrible muddle and don't know what to do. All I know is that I can't stand it much longer. Ever since Mary's mother has been here I've been going through hell. I thought England was bad enough, but this is a thousand times worse. At least back home the woman had her own house and circle of friends. Here she's on top of us all the time. I feel I can't do a damn thing without her disapproving. She treats me as some kind of freak who has to be tolerated because I know no better. If only she'd explode, tell me what's wrong, say what she thinks, but no, nothing—she sits on her dignity and now and again, I can't help myself, and I'm rude to her. I tell you Dave I don't feel I'm living in my own house. Then it all leads to dreadful rows with Mary. She tells me I'm imagining things and that really I ought to treat her mother with more respect... Well, I can't stand it any longer. I've done my best. I can't do more. Maybe Mary is right, I'm not seeing straight? I don't know what she expects me to do. Frankly I've been toying with the idea of leaving her."

"You're not serious," cried Payton shaken from his calm.

"Dead serious. Couldn't be more so. I've already made most of the arrangements." He then said he had been making enquiries about a job in Jamaica and yesterday he'd got a letter accepting him. "I've got to give them an answer before the end of the week. I think they've got some other bod up their sleeve and they don't' want to turn him down until they've got something definite from me." He then went on to say that he knew it would be hard on Mary, but he couldn't take any more. "I'll send Mary my address when I'm settled in a month or two. I'll make it quite clear that Lady Shackleton mustn't follow her."

"Why don't you tell Mary now?"

"Maybe I will. I'm so confused I don't know what to do."

Payton's mind was in a whirl. All the while Frith had been talking he had been thinking. He hadn't seen Peter for more than ten years. He didn't really know him. He had taken everything the man had said at face value. It struck him that Lady Shackleton might know something he didn't. The train of his thoughts compelled him to be blunt: "Is there another woman?" he asked.

Frith's jaw dropped. He stared incredulously at Payton.

"I'm sorry. I shouldn't have said that."

There was an awkward pause.

"Really Dave. I don't know what you must think of me? You make me feel a positive heel. I thought you were my friend."

Again Payton apologized. He said that he too was mixed up. He didn't know what to think. Then he told him what Lady Shakleton had said.

"That woman is capable of anything," Frith replied.

Pause.

"Is it true?" Payton pressed gently.

After a moment's silence he said: "Yes, it's true all right. But how the hell did she get to know?" He hesitated before going on and when he did he spoke quickly: "Hell Dave, what's a fellow to do? I'll swear to you that there's no other woman in my life besides Mary. But now and again I just can't help myself. I'm human. It would have been worse if I'd had a regular girl. That would have shown some attachment. But with these other women there was nothing: just a screw. I tell you the only girl who means anything to me is Mary."

"You still love her then?"

"Of course I do. It's just her mother. I can't stand her. If I'm around her much longer I don't hold myself responsible for my actions."

"You'll break Mary's heart if you leave her."

"I know. I hate myself. But things can't go on as they are. I'll kill the woman if I have to put up with her much longer."

"Listen Peter. It's none of my business I know, but I don't want to see your marriage break up. Why don't you go away for a few weeks? Think things over. Maybe when you return you'll see things differently."

"And what about the job I've got lined up in Jamaica? My work here has been suffering and I know they're not too pleased with me. I don't want to end up with nothing."

"What's more important Mary or your job?"

"Oh David, I know you mean well, but really you're not getting it. Both go together. As it is Lady Shackleton thinks I am supporting her daughter in a style she in unaccustomed to. If I had no means of support that would be the end. If you have any advice you should give it to my mother-in-law. Tell her to quit meddling in our lives. Ever since we've been married she's tried to come between us. I really don't understand her. Once we were married what point was there? She could have given us her blessings, and left it at that, even if she didn't approve of the marriage."

Payton shook his head: "I'm afraid old boy you're missing Lady Shackleton's point. As far as she 's concerned she's not trying to break up your marriage. She simply wants to be with Mary because she thinks you'll let her down. She also thinks that her presence asserts a sobering influence on you."

Frith cut in angrily. "Like hell she does. That's all rot and you know it. The woman has done all she can to separate us from the very beginning?"

"If that's how you feel you're not going to let her succeed by going away are you?"

Frith threw his head back, his lips tightened and he stuck his chin out. "Hell man, you're right. I hadn't thought of it that way. I'm not going to be defeated by that bloody woman."

Payton then went on to re-enforce his argument. He said they'd both regret it if they split up. He had little doubt that Lady Shackleton's attitude would change when she saw he really loved Mary. He was going through a difficult phase. All marriages had their tribulations. He mustn't give up. By the time they parted Payton felt that he had persuaded Frith from acting too hastily.

Days passed and Payton didn't hear a word from the Friths. Several times he had been tempted to phone, but had refrained as their personal affairs were really none of his business. Then one morning when he got to the office he found a letter waiting for him.

Dear Dave,

By the time you get this letter I shall be in Jamaica. I'm sorry I couldn't see you before leaving, but I just hadn't the courage. Everything you said the other day was absolutely right and when I left you I was resolved to stick things out; but then a couple of days more with my mother-in-law and I just couldn't face it. I simply had to get out. It was all very well you giving me a thousand good reasons why I should stay. I know you meant well. I appreciate your support, but the fact is that I had to put up with the woman and you didn't.

I just left Mary a good-bye note. I didn't tell her where I was going and I should be grateful if you didn't either. In due course I'll probably drop her a line and let her know what to do. In the mean time please look after her and try and explain that what I've done is all for the best.

Then, I knew they weren't too pleased with me at the job. I think they wanted to get rid of me anyway, so when I gave my notice and asked to leave early they didn't object. The job in Jamaica is a better one, I'm sure of that. In a month or two I expect I'll see things clearer. I'll write to you again then. In the mean time all the best. Thanks for everything. You've been a brick. Hope you don't think too badly of me.

Your friend

Pete

Payton read the letter again and immediately called Mary. It was several minutes before she answered. She was in a terrible state and he had difficulty understanding her. She said her husband had walked out on her. Yes, there was a note. Just two lines. She read them:

I'm sorry darling I'm leaving you. I can't stand it any longer. Please forgive me. Love Pete.

The word "it" was underlined. Then, as far as he could make out, she'd had a row with her mother. She'd told her to her face she was to blame.

"Now I'm on my own. Mother's gone out for a while. She says she quite understands how I feel and that what I need is a little quiet and rest. She realizes that, at the moment, she gets on my nerves: that later I'll need her and I'll be only too pleased to have her around." She then asked him to come to the house as soon possible. "Right away. I'll hop in the car and be with you within the hour. There's not much I have to do at the office today.

In a very short time she was opening the door to him. He followed her into the lounge and sat down. The place was bright and modern, air-conditioned. Mary in a white dress looked collected. He didn't know what to say. His inclination was to say the usual things: how sorry he was, she didn't deserve it, he never thought it would happen, maybe things would work out. But somehow the words stuck in his throat. She served him a rum and coke.

"I'm thinking of following him. I know he needs me. I don't know where he's gone, but it shouldn't be too difficult to check the airlines. Did he, by any chance, tell you anything?"

Payton hesitated, then replied: "I got a letter from him this morning. He says he'll be writing to you shortly. He needs a little time to think things over."

She asked if she could see the letter.

"I'm afraid I left it at the office."

"Mummy says I'm well rid of him. She thinks I'd be humiliating myself if I chased after him and then it would be a terrible shock to me if I discovered he was with another woman. That's what started the row. I said Pete wasn't like that. The idea was absurd. I was very annoyed at even the suggestion. Then, when mummy went on to ask what possible other reason there was I exploded. I was very blunt. I told her it was all her fault. I spared her nothing."

She stopped abruptly and stifled a sob.

"And what did she say to that?" asked Payton.

Mary wiped her eyes and cheeks.

"She said I was saying a lot of things I didn't mean. She knew Peter didn't like her, but she was sorry to see that he'd poisoned my mind against her as well. If I chose to believe all my husband told me there was nothing she could do. Maybe with a little rest and quiet reflection I 'd see things differently."

She paused and threw Payton a quick searching look. "Tell me Dave you know Pete so well, is it true what mummy says? I want to know. I have a right to know. Don't worry about sparing my feelings."

"I wish I knew the answer," Payton replied.

"You don't honestly believe that Peter has run off with another woman?"

He shook his head. "No. If you want my personal opinion he still loves you. And all he says about your mother he believes is true. I'm not saying it is, but that is what he thinks. In the same way your mother is just as convinced that her impressions of Peter are true."

Mary smiled. "I hoped you'd say that. It's exactly how I feel. Now, it won't be as bad if I eventually decide to follow him. Of course I'll have to tell mummy not to come after me and she won't be able to see me as often. It'll be hard on her to start with, but I know she loves me and really wants my happiness."

Payton nodded and although he thought Mary's idea of happiness wasn't the same as her mother's he didn't say so. Instead he said: "It's a very tough decision you'll have to make."

She gave a faint smile. "I've made it. I know where my happiness lies. Peter needs me and I need him. We've always been happy together. Of course I love mummy very much; but I'm a grown woman and have my own life to lead."

At that moment Lady Shackleton came in the room.

"Ah, Mr Payton, delighted to see you again. It's been months since I saw you." She offered him her delicate hand and sat down.

Lady Shackleton was wearing a light blue dress, brown walking shoes and had a long bead necklace which came down over her chest. She had a light tan and looked the picture of health. If she was suffering from the heat and humidity she showed no signs of it.

She began talking about this and that. She asked Payton about his trip, whether he had met any interesting people and if he was pleased to be back in Port of Spain. Then she switched to talking about her impressions of Trinidad. She liked it more than she expected. It was a very colorful place. She was fascinated by the intermingling of the races. She loved the Colonial architecture. She had been to San Fernando and La Brea Point, where the Asphalt Lake was. The process was very interesting, she thought. Payton, all the while sat silent, as did Mary who fidgeted nervously and looked glum and angry. Eventually, it seemed that she could take no more of her mother's idle banter and rose and stormed towards the door.

"Darling, don't go. If I'm boring you I'll leave. You can stay and chat with Mr Payton."

Mary stopped. "I'm sorry mummy. I'm just not in the mood."

"Darling," the older lady purred. "I wanted to take your mind off yourself. It's not good to brood over ones problems. It only makes them worse."

"I wanted to tell you what I'd decided."

"Well dear?"

Mary spoke fast as though she wanted to get it over with. "I'm going to join Pete. He needs me. I know he can't do without me."

Mary searched her mother's face for some sign of approval. Lady Shackleton wore a Poker face.

"Really dear. I didn't know you had his address."

"I haven't, but I soon will. Dave got a letter from Pete this morning. He'll be writing to me shortly. I'm not sure whether I should wait to hear from him or go right away."

Lady Shackleton replied as though she had been asked a question: "Do as you like dear. I won't try and persuade you one way or the other."

"You don't approve then?"

"I can't see what difference it makes what I think. You've been quite content not to listen to me from the very start."

Mary went a little red. "Oh mummy how can you say that? You know perfectly well I've always done my best to please you. It's just that recently Pete and I don't seem to do anything right."

"I've always done what I thought was in your best interest."

"Yes mummy, I know. You've been an angel; but sometimes you do presume to know better than I do what's good for me. Won't you for once give me the benefit of the doubt? Tell me to go to Pete. Give me your blessings. Admit that you could be wrong."

Mary was giving her mother a supplicating look. Lady Shackleton was unmoved: "Darling, you wouldn't want me to tell you one thing if I thought another? I couldn't possibly encourage you to follow Peter if I didn't think you should."

"You won't do it then?" Mary spoke softly with tears in her eyes. She lingered a moment, as though hoping and giving her mother a chance to change her mind. When, however, there was no reply, she burst into tears and fled the room.

For a minute or two nothing was said, then Lady Shackleton spoke: "It's very hard on her now poor dear, but she'll get over it. Time is a great healer. Between you and me Mr Payton she is well rid of him. I knew it would come to this and thank God I'm here when she needs me."

"That's what you always wanted isn't it?" Payton said sullenly.

"Yes. I knew that sooner or later he'd run off with another woman."

"But how do you know that's what he's done?"

Lady Shackleton smiled: "I don't, but everything points that way. And even if he hasn't this time he will one day. People don't change their spots you know."

Payton stifled a gasp. "But don't you want them to make up if it's at all possible?"

Again she gave her disarming smile. "I think we've been through that before Mr Payton. I'm a realist. I don't believe in miracles. You can't change peoples' origins. I tell you that marriages outside one's class don't work."

Payton gave Lady Shackleton a hard look. He knew then that only death could defeat her.

Meanwhile, lying on her bed, Mary wept.

Travel

Nassau: No Thank You

Like me he came to Nassau because he thought he might live here. We met in the library. He was a medium sized man with a bullet of a head, almost bald. I should say somewhere in his sixties. About him there was an air of a Colonial---conservative, propertied with red cheeks, though he didn't drink.

That first meeting I did most of the talking. England was my complaint: decadence, socialism, impoverishment; how the mighty had fallen. My intention was to get out while the going was good. Or if I didn't get out I at least intended to get my money out.

The Colonial gentleman agreed with every word I said, though things weren't as bad for him as he lived in Jersey. But he had the weather to complain about. The weather in Jersey was no better than in England.

Two days later I again met this gentleman in the library. He told me he had definitely decided he wasn't going to stay in The Bahamas. "I don't know how I could have ever thought I was going to live here."

"What has made you decide so quickly?" I asked.

"Well, I went to the pictures last night. I like going to the pictures. But these little black devils spoil everything. I just couldn't hear what was being said most of the time. The noise. Bottles, jeers, screams. And then when they laugh they go on for ages. It ruins the film. They've got their own cinemas. There are three of theirs and two of ours. I don't think the little devils should be allowed in. Well, that definitely decided it for me. There are no theaters here and if I can't go to the cinemas there's nothing for me. No, this place is not for me. I'm pleased I've come to a decision. I don't know how I ever thought I could live here."

"You're lucky to have decided so quickly. It must be a relief to know what you're going to do."

He nodded: "Oh, I could never stick this place. I went to Freeport a little while ago. Never again. No thank you. I know I shall never see the place as long as I live. All modern, commercialized, dreadful. This place is going exactly the same way. American. They're killing the place."

"They are bringing in the money."

"Let them. It's not for me. I know that now. It was a great mistake for me to come here. But we all make mistakes don't we? I shan't come back here again. I just want to stick the winter out. I want the sun, but the price isn't worth it. I know what I'm going to do. I'll spend six months in Jersey and for the winter I'll go to Madeira. I'm pleased I've made up my mind, I don't know how I could have ever thought I was going to live here."

He then told me about the flat he had just moved into. "What a mess they left it in. A proper big devil is that landlord. He said it would be all spic and span when I moved in. There were two messy girls in there before. I think he was fooling around with them. Dirty little man. And he charges £55. I told him that he'd have to get the place cleaned up before I moved in. I wasn't going to stand any of his nonsense, nasty little man. I was right wasn't I? If you pay you expect to get something for it."

"£55 doesn't sound too expensive for here."

"How much are you paying for your place?"

"£47."

"Oh you are, are you? I tried to get a cheaper place but I just couldn't find one. This was the first place that came along and I just took it. I was very lucky to get it."

It was 1:30 and I suggested lunch.

"No thank you. I have my cheese and biscuits."

A few days later I had a look over his flat. It opened out on to an external corridor. No view, though a little more light than my place which only had two windows: one over-looking a brick wall, the other a car junk yard. He had a little kitchenette, bathroom, bedroom and the entrance, small, was his lounge. Stone floor. A cheap canape, a couple of chairs, a table and that was about the lot, furniture-wise.

"He's a little devil that man. I've asked him for a bath mat three or four times and he keeps saying 'yes' and never brings it. What these people will try and get out of. There should have been a bath mat before I came into the flat. He won't spend a penny, mean old rascal. I'm getting to know these people. All I want to do is to hang on till March."

I suggested he get to know a few people: it might change his ideas a bit.

"Oh, I don't want to know anybody. I know what they're like. I know the ex-governor or secretary. I don't know exactly what he is. A pompous little so and so: a nasty piece of work. His wife's charming. I don't know how she married him. I've rang him up three times and I never find him in. So I went along to his office. He wanted to know my number and I told him I hadn't a phone. Had it taken out in fact. I don't want a phone. I've got nobody to ring up and there's nobody to ring me up. If he was busy I told him I'd ring up another day. I've rung up twice and each time he's been out. Well, I wasn't going to go chasing after him any more I can tell you that. I told his secretary if he wanted to get in touch with me he should leave a note with the librarian. He hasn't, of course. He doesn't want to see me I'm sure of that. I don't think he approves of my not wearing a jacket. But I'm not going to wear a jacket for him. And I don't really want to see him anyway. Terrible bore. And I'd have to invite him round to this little prison. I wouldn't like to do that. He's got a lovely place somewhere out East. No, I'm quite happy on my own. I don't need anybody. If I've got the pictures that's enough for me. I potter about the rest of the time. I can fill my day, I don't need that stuffed shirt to introduce me to anybody."

"Were you ever married?" I shot out.

"Oh, no, quite enough trouble looking after myself. I wouldn't want any more baggage. Never wanted to get married. Not for me. No thank you."

"Have you any brothers or sisters?"

"I had a brother. Drunk himself to death. Died at 63. He was a very odd man. Even as his brother I say that. Didn't do a stroke of work in his life. Hated the Jews. Thought Hitler should have bumped off the lot. He admired the dictators: Franco, Hitler, Mussolini. But I think he may have repented in the end. He left some of his money to charity, just imagine. He only did it because he couldn't bear the idea of the government getting most of the money. Nor me for that matter. He wouldn't like it one little bit if he knew I'd got much of it. I was lucky wasn't I? Very odd man was my brother."

"What did he do with his life? Did he have any hobbies or anything?"

"Oh no, nothing at all, just drunk himself to death."

"What about yourself? Are you retired or something?"

"I retired twenty years ago on May the 5th."He quickly added: "I'm not 80 or anything like that. Just had enough of work so I quit. That's why I went to Jersey. Wasn't going to have the government helping themselves to my money. Oh no, that wasn't for me. Jersey is only fifty five minutes away from London. I can go there when I want. Never bored in London. Go to the theater every night. There are all the cinemas I need. This place is much too far from England, I should have known that, but I've I learnt my lesson, I'll never come back here again. Never."

"I wish I'd decided what I was going to do. I'd hoped to meet some people here."

"You won't, you know."

"I'm beginning to think you're right. I thought that after six weeks I would have met some people."

"I could have told you you wouldn't. I'm pleased I've decided. I was silly to think I could live here." Etc. etc.

The next time I saw him was the Sunday before Christmas. I had nothing to do and knowing he wasn't mobile, dropped in at his place and asked him if he'd like to go for a drive round the island.

As soon as we were in the car he told me of his latest decision. He wasn't going to wait until March; he was going to clear out sooner. "January 16th," he beamed. "I can't wait to get out of this place quick enough. I'm counting the days. I don't know how I'm going to face this next week. But I thought I had better get Christmas over with. It would be just as bad arriving somewhere else at Christmas. But I'm pleased I've made up my mind. The next week is going to be awful, I know that. I shall remember my stay here until the end of my days." On he jabbered, the same old routine. Inadvertently he told me he was going to Palm Beach. "At least I'll have the cinemas there,"

"I don't understand if you're so set against this place why you don't leave sooner?"

"Believe me I would if I could. But I had to give that little rascal his month's notice. Do you know he hasn't brought me my mat yet? Little devil. Every time I see him I point to the floor and he knows exactly what I mean. But it doesn't matter now.

"I don't suppose I'll ever get it. I was speaking to the woman in the Tourist Office and she knows him. 'He used to be such a nice young man,' she says. I think she knows all about him. He's up at the flats, messing around with the girls every night. Dancing, drinking, making a filthy racket. The girls are just prostitutes. White girls. Do you know that one of them came in here to borrow my mop, stark naked. They are just prostitutes, I don't know how many they are. I know there are two next to me and I think there are another two further down the corridor.

"Well, it's not for long now. I'll just have face the next few weeks. It has been done hasn't it? It's not going to be nice I know that. I thought of moving somewhere else, closer to the beach. Silly of me, I knew I shouldn't have bothered. The Verger at the church gave me an address. A black man. He knew which side his bread was buttered, wicked little man. Said the place would cost £50, the little rascal. He though he would get away with it. He didn't know who he had to deal with. I rang Mrs. Smith and do you know she wanted only £35. He knew that of course. You can't trust these people. I've never met people more dishonest. And they're nothing. Bahamian. Nothing at all. And they think so much of themselves, silly little nits. Anyway, the flat was gone. Sly little devil. He didn't want to see me after that. Saw him hiding behind one of the pillars when I passed the church. He thought I hadn't seen him. But it's not for much longer. I'll soon be out of this place. You won't stay you know, I'm sure of that. At one time I thought you'd be out before me."

"I've decided nothing."

"I'm just counting the days. But only three more weeks. I get quite jolly when I think about it. Did I tell you about when I went into the Riviera—that's the restaurant? I don't think they like me there. I've been in the place three times and each time walked out. If there's nothing on the menu that I like I'm not going to stay. You wouldn't, would you? Then, there's the assistant cook or something. He's only 19: he hates the place. American boy. Terrified of the boss. He's much bigger than him, he says. He told me never to go into the place. Killed seven rats with a knife, he said, would you believe it? Fairly turned my stomach. 'Don't you have any sanitary inspectors here,' I asked? He said I ought to see the cleaning board, hadn't been washed for months.

"I used to go to the Grand Central, but not now, no more. The waitress knew I was in a hurry. I knew she didn't like me, I could tell that. They are a sly lot, wicked. She deliberately wouldn't serve me: kept me waiting for fifteen minutes. I called the manager over. He was very polite I must say, but I'm not going back. No thank you.

"They're so silly these people. They've got no brains at all. They don't listen to you. Would you believe it, the manager took the wrong order! Stupid man. Not much good being apologetic is it? They're nothing these Bahamians. Nothing at all. I only consider them half a brain. Nits. I only go to the Poinciana now, at least they're polite there."

"It's a good thing you're not here very long as you'd probably find yourself with nowhere to eat."

He laughed: "That's right. But only three more weeks. Aren't I pleased to be leaving. I shall never forget my stay here." (We were now passing Government House.) "Oh, there's Government House. Have you signed the book, the visitor's book?"

"No. What's the point of that?" I asked.

"They invite you to a cocktail or something. They never do of course. I've signed the book three times and never been invited once."

"Shall we all the same?. We lose nothing by trying."

I pulled up and we duly crossed the road and went to the little hut which contained the visitor's book. We signed.

"Won't do any good, I can promise you that," he said, as he got into the car.

For a short while we rode in silence. We were going down Shirley Street towards East Bay where you find the luxurious homes, how the rich live. Soon we were going down Eastern Road (the same as East Bay Street).The road was rotten, but the homes lay back in a kind of resplendent voluptuousness of trimmed hedges, palms and poincianas. Very relaxing. Very beautiful. Spacious. And to crown it all a magnificent blue sky and, though December, the temperature in the mid-seventies. For a moment I had visions of London, grey, cold, wet. Already there had been snow in November."Well, we've at least got the weather and the scenery to be thankful for," I said.

"It's an expensive price to pay. There's nothing better than one's own country really. I know that now. I was silly to think otherwise. Still, we all make mistakes don't we? I've paid very dearly for this one. I'd go mad if I stayed in my little prison. But I wasn't going to clear out once I'd paid; that would be foolish of me. Wasn't going to let that little rascal get my money for nothing. Did I tell you my tap sprung a leak and I had to ask him to call the plumber? I gave him what for, the silly man. 'Mr. Jackson,' I said, 'I've asked you three times for the plumber and still he hasn't come.' I pointed down at my feet and he knew exactly what I meant. The stupid man then told me the plumber had been and each time I'd been out. 'He should wait for me,' I said. That's how it should be,

I'm not going to be at the beck and call of the plumber. That's right isn't it? If he thinks I've got nothing better to do than hang around my little prison all day waiting for the plumber he's even stupider than I think. He thinks he's a bright spark, but with me he must be learning fast. He's not going to get the better of me. Well, it worked, for when I came in from the library the plumber and his boy were waiting on the verandah. Oh they made a horrible mess and his boy seemed horribly sleepy: Sitting down all the time, on my chairs his eyes closed, yawning. I don't think anything beats these Bahamians for laziness. I've never seen anything like it. Anyway, I got what I wanted; but I had to clean up after they'd gone. I do it once a week. I'd only done it the day before. Three more clean-ups and I'm off. Perhaps I won't clean up the last week, let the little rascal pay some woman to do it for him. I don't think he's ever had a tenant like me. But he's a nasty piece of work. He gets me mad." (What he has to say next makes me almost piss in my pants.) "But it's a good thing I've got a sense of humor. It's all very funny when you think about it. If you're determined to see the jolly side of things you always can. You can always win, that's right, isn't it?"

We were now returning back to the center of town."That's one of the places I saw," he continued, interrupting himself and pointing to a rather ramshackle building. "A colored woman owns the place, though she won't admit she's colored. Silly isn't it? You can't change what you are. A very depressing place. She's got seven children, yelling and screaming just like ants. As soon as I saw that I said the place wasn't for me. No thank you. Horrible little creatures. A man there said they were only visiting. I expect they visited every day."

"Well, here we are," I said, bringing the car to a halt. I left him to return to his den. For Christmas I put a card under his door. HOPE YOU HAVE A VERY HAPPY CHRISTMAS and inside SOMEHOW.

That evening when I returned from a dinner engagement there was an envelope stuck in the glass of my door. It was a Christmas card and it was signed Ralph Borr. Who the hell is Ralph Borr I wondered? It struck me that the card wasn't for me at all, but my predecessor. I left it at that.

The next time I saw the Colonial gentleman was on Boxing day. I was having a snack in the Howard Johnson at the Nassau Beach Hotel, when suddenly I caught sight of him. He had just gone in the main entrance. He looked very excited, all in a dither. I would have known something was wrong even if I hadn't seen his face. The Nassau Beach is five miles out of town and I knew he wouldn't have made the journey for nothing. My curiosity was aroused and I beckoned the waitress to bring my bill. A moment or two later, and before she had brought it, he came into the restaurant. I saw him chat with the manageress. Then they went to one of the tables and started searching, under the table, on the seats, here and there. I could just make out what he was saying. "It's no use, they've gone. They'll never be found, I know that. I think I lost them in Church. They've been taken, sure as Punch. No question about it."

"What have you lost?" I said, joining him.

"My glasses. I came here yesterday with the woman from the Tourist Office before going to Church. But I know they are not here. I lost them in the Church. I'm positive of that. I spent the whole morning looking for them. I saw that horrible little Verger again. He wasn't pleased to see me I can tell you that. Oh well, it's no use going on looking, I know they are not here."

"I don't see why anybody should take your glasses," I said. "What would they do with them?"

"It's not the glasses they would have taken the little devils, it's the case. It's a nice case. It's worth something. They'd do anything for money, I know that. Oh well, it'll only mean that I can't go to the cinema until March."

I smothered a giggle. "Haven't you got another pair?" I asked.

"No, I don't bother with that."

"I'm sure you could have some made here if you really wanted."

"Oh no, won't bother. They wouldn't make them properly anyway."

I offered him a lift back to town. In the car he started at once: "I loathe this place. I'll never forget my stay here until the end of my days. I can't even sleep properly now. The people opposite me have gone away for Christmas and a beastly little woman has taken over the flat. She's got a dog that yaps all night. Beastly little animal. I'd like to wring its neck. And then those tarts next door. They're so stupid. I think they're Canadian. Shop girls. Nothing at all. Jabber. Jabber. Jabber. You ought to hear some of the balderdash they talk. One of them was baking a cake and burnt it. Silly nit. If she didn't want it to burn she should have watched it. Oh well, not much longer now: exactly three weeks. I'm just waiting for the day. I'll never set foot in this place again. No thank you. By the way, did you get my card?"

"Your card?... Oh yes, your card, thank you very much."

Ralph Borr, I thought. What an appropriate name.

St. Thomas

I went to St. Thomas by the *Flying Fish*--- in fact something like a flying fish, long, thin with a pointed nose and fins to keep the spray down. I took the boat from Fajardo on the north east coast of Puerto Rico. The boat shot across the water like a torpedo skimming the surface of the water. I reckon we were traveling between 30 and 40 m.p.h. We bumped furiously, not because it was rough, but because we were going so fast. The waves came racing towards us, lashing us from every side, throwing spray into the passenger compartment. All around us were little islands, rocks and cays. I was fascinated by their shapes, coloring and in the distance the blue-green haze of mountain contours. Overhead hung threatening rain clouds, but I was told "not to worry", it never rained in The Virgins Islands and anyway it wasn't even the rainy season. Now and again, when the spray got too fierce we slowed, or sometimes we didn't, but simply changed direction so that the waves would hit us at a different angle.

Gradually the little island of St. Thomas loomed larger. It was early evening and we could see the undulating hills, green with trees of every shade, with here and there patches of rock or beach reflecting streaks of light. Soon we picked out the white water traps[1] amidst the greenery, then a church spire, roof tops, a tower, whole houses. Hilly islets were speckled about the sea. We were going quite slowly now and we wended our way in and out of these. Eventually the little wharf was in front of us. We could see people gathering there. This was Charlotte Amalie, the one and only town on the island and capital of St. Thomas.

The Virgins were so named by Columbus in 1493. He had been to St. Thomas and I later saw the exact spot where he apparently first

---

[1] Water traps looked like white sheets spread across the mountain sides. However, they acted more like large bath tubs, for their purpose was to store water as it rarely rained in the Virgins.

landed. (All the islands I subsequently discovered had a speck of beach where Columbus first landed!) At the time of the discovery the island was inhabited by Carib and Arawak Indians.

St. Thomas had been the gateway between the old and new world: New England sailing captains traded barrel staves for rum and sugar; pirates skulked the island looting for Inca gold bound for the Spanish Main; ships from everywhere put in at St. Thomas first to refuel and later, when the trans-Atlantic cable was laid, to receive instructions. Slavery thrived on the island and for thirty years it was the biggest slave market in the world.

St. Thomas was successively owned by British, French, Dutch, Spanish and Danes. In 1917 it was bought by the United States for $25 million. Although the island had been occupied by the English for a very short time, English had been the spoken language for a very long time. Apparently this was because the overseers had always been English.

The island was at present administered by the Department of Interior with the Governor appointed by the President of the U.S.

I met M.P. on the Flying Fish. He was Swiss and spoke both English and French and like me was a seasoned traveler. We decided to see the island together.

After quickly settling in at a hotel we roamed about Charlotte's Amalie's quaint tortuous cobbled little streets. It fascinated us to see Danish street names, driving on the left hand side of the road, although in an American Trust Territory. We liked the small shops without display windows, but doors wide open as though to say "welcome, come in". The impression we got was of a quality street sale with the merchandise luring us in, as though it was a signpost for something better inside. St. Thomas was a free port. We moved from shop to shop: the French Shoppe, the Spanish Main, Maison Danoise, Scandinavian Silver, the London Shoppe, Little Switzerland. Cameras, Swiss watches, French perfumes, wines, twin-sets, silverware and much more— were abundantly displayed. There were bargains galore. Temptation was everywhere, but we were counting our pennies and restrained ourselves. We stopped for a snack. We didn't eat much, but what we had was pricy. If the luxuries were cheap the necessities made up for it by being horrendously expensive.

Then we did the things tourists do. We went to Government House, signed the visitor's book, saw the famous 99 steps, climbed to the top of a hill and looked around Blue Beard's Tower, an ex-pirate haunt. We went to a fort, church, synagogue, the local market place. We visited French Town where we pitted our French against the native Patoi. We had a grand time. We liked everything and everybody. The natives were very friendly and, though quite black, were mostly devoid of negroid features. They were tall with thin lips and slender noses. The girls had lovely figures and did not get fat after twenty like so many Bahamanian women. The people spoke a Calypso English, rhythmic and bouncy like their dancing. Both M.P. and I liked them.

That evening we went to the Virgin Isle Hotel. We were told it was one of the finest in the two Americas. It certainly had all the amenities and situated on high ground the view was splendid. But we had come to see the turtle races. The turtles were put in little wooden box-like compartments at one end of the pool. On the word "GO" one side of the compartments was slid open and the turtles paddled off. They didn't always head towards the finish line. In fact in many cases they seemed to move quite randomly. I noticed that this was particularly the case when the pool was lit up on all sides. Later, I discovered that turtles were attracted by light and that was the incentive for them head towards it. Needless to say, when the side beacons were on, the races lasted much longer. It was all great fun and though we lost a little money betting, it was all for a good cause as proceeds went to the local hospital fund.

However, the real highlight of St. Thomas for both of us was its scenery. Twenty four hours before our scheduled departure we hired a car and toured the island. By hiring the car exactly a day before we were due to leave we saved ourselves a taxi fare to the airport, for we had arranged with the agent that he should collect the car there. It is difficult to describe St. Thomas's scenic beauty, for, like a work of art, the sum of the parts is less than the whole. Green hills, tropical trees, white deserted beaches, an azure and blue-green sea, clean fresh air—-we had seen it all before; but somehow St. Thomas had an indescribable something more. Or maybe it was just us: we had enjoyed our stay immensely; we were relaxed and happy, at peace with the world. Perhaps it was simply our mood that made us see St. Thomas's beauty as we did

Guadaloupe

If you are going to Guadeloupe and have made only the most meager enquiries about accommodation you will undoubtedly have heard Mario. Mario is the proprietor of the Pergola, a hotel just outside Pointe a Pitre and in the fashionable area of Gosier.

I had heard all sorts of strange and uncomplimentary things about Mario: he was rogue, a thief, his prices were exorbitant and he would rob you of your last penny, but nevertheless, I was told, I simply must visit. It was with a mixture of curiosity and trepidation that I got into a taxi and told the driver to take me to the Pergola.

The Pergola was on top of a small hillock commanding a splendid view of the sea and the little island of *Ilet du Gosier*. On the island, peeping up above the trees you could see a red and white lighthouse. At night this lighthouse winked at you in bright red.

The entrance to the hotel faced a kind of private square where residents, visitors and of course Monsieur Mario parked their cars. The Pergola itself was small, white and very much like a new gas station with its back wall blown out: it was here that Mario had his splendid verandah where he served his guests with food and drink at fashionable prices.

I got out of the taxi and surveyed the scene a little closer: on the porch stood a naked woman carved in wood, Mexican style; her hands clasped self-consciously over her crotch. On her head was a stuffed red, blue and yellow parrot that stared at me fixedly with round beady eyes. I threaded my way into the entrance between a couple of rusty antique cannon barrels that lay sticking outwards away from the porch. As I did so, I was a little taken aback, for the parrot, which I had thought stuffed, turned its head and stared at me. Then a huge and fine looking Alsatian

135

appeared from nowhere, came up to me and began   sniffing me suspiciously, as though he wanted to make sure that I could afford Mario's prices. I did not sign a register, but was taken straightaway to my pergolette, a bedroom   cum bathroom bungalow—all clean and comfortable looking.

After a wash and brush up I had a further look around. I met the Persian cat that sleeps on a wicker chair twenty four hours a day. (Later I learned it was so lazy that it did nothing more strenuous than shift from one chair to the next, and that only when it was disturbed from the first.) I met two tiny green parrots that walked up and down the bar counter like a couple of sentries on guard. Guy, who I could not quite make out but surmised was Mario's right-hand man, said one of them was friendly, but the other bites. As they looked exactly alike this information wasn't much help.

"Do they speak?" I asked.

"One of them speaks a little Spanish," replied Guy and then after a pause went on to tell me that Mario had a third green parrot that spoke French, but a plate fell on its head and it died. Guy was a slender young man with a long face and brown melancholy eyes. He was always about when I, or anybody else for that matter, wanted him and although he looked sad when alone perked up the moment you spoke to him. Somehow he reminded me of a hungry student. He lingered in the background as I examined more of Mario's curios.

Mario's verandah was in its own way like a small museum. On the walls there were pictures of pirates, ancient and modern maps of Guadeloupe, rusty swords and daggers and here and there a rifle suspended from a hook. On the floor there were cannon balls in varying sizes, several ships steering wheels, a cage and in it a queer looking bird with a long beak which I feel certain only an ornithologist could name. It was while I was looking at Mario's curios that I came across *Peepo*. Later, I was surprised that I hadn't met him earlier for he had a knack of being exactly where he shouldn't be and was a monstrous show off. He would perform all sorts of clever tricks, act the fool, do this and that and make a thorough nuisance of himself. You would always be quite sure of finding him in precisely where he shouldn't be. *Peepo* was a monkey.

Guy told me that *Peepo* was very friendly and that there was no danger—I could pat him and take him on my shoulder if I wanted. In order to show that I was not a coward and that I was fond of animals I did what was suggested. I quickly learnt, to my detriment, that *Peepo* was only too friendly: in an instant he had taken off my glasses and rendered me helpless, he clicked my camera, pulled some buttons off my shirt and started fiddling around in my pockets while dangling from my neck by his tail. As soon as I could I checked for my wallet. Thankfully it was still there, though I didn't check the contents. *Peepo* was so friendly that I wouldn't have been in the least bit surprised if he'd emptied it for me.

"At one time he used to like getting into people's cars and helping himself to whatever he could find in them; but we soon put a stop to that by locking the doors." Guy paused and without so much as a flicker of a smile went on: "When we did that *Peepo* took to dismantling the windscreen wipers and deflating the tires as though he had to avenge himself for the pleasure we had deprived him.

" Peepo is very bright. For instance, a little while ago he did something wrong and was due for a spanking and knowing this grabbed a nearby kitten that was in the yard and hid under the refrigerator. Every time we tried to get hold of him he presented us with the kitten as though it, and not him, was due for the punishment."

By lunch time I had seen Mario's private beach, a stone chute by the Pergolettes in which you could slide into the sea, more monkeys, parrots, a dear, a hog and a few other animals. I still had not met Mario, but was beginning to know something about him as I had seen many of his possessions.

It was while I was at lunch that Mario made his grand entry. Normally I would have seen him earlier, but today he had gone shopping in Pointe-a-Pitre and our meeting was delayed.

If, as Shakespeare suggests, the world is but a stage and we are all actors on it, Mario fitted his part admirably. He was short, brisk and businesslike. He wore grey flannels, a white shirt with short sleeves and on his head had a ridiculous straw hat that didn't suit him at all. Mario was somewhere in his forties: his face was lined, his cheeks were gently red and his nose hooked like one of his parrots. He had friendly emerald eyes which appeared to observe nothing and yet, I soon discovered, saw everything. Mario was all things to all men: he had the charm of Charles Boyer and the cunning of a Machiavelli; he appeared to be as adaptable as a Chameleon.

While people lunched he went from table to table. I saw him in a variety of moods: one moment he was serious, probably discussing business or politics; the next he was laughing, feeding one of his clients infants or playing with *Peepo* who had suddenly turned up to see what trouble he might make. Or again I would hear him rapping out an order: he had seen a client beckon a waiter; but before she had time to say what she wanted Mario has called out: "Madam needs a fork"; "Madam wants an ash tray", or "There is no water on Madam's table".

Mario has a kind of sixth sense: he knew exactly what his guests wanted (or perhaps he even knew their thoughts) before they ever opened their mouths. He was never so tactless as to enquire whether the food was good or not for he instinctively knew whether a client was pleased or dissatisfied. If anybody surreptitiously whispered to the friend sharing his table that the meat was not all it should be he discovered that the next time he ate at the Pergola the meat was extra good. The longer a person stayed at his place the more conscious he became of this uncanny power of premonition. It was disconcerting I must say. I somehow felt that it was impossible to hide anything from Mario. I wondered where he got his strange powers from and I was eager to find out more about him.

Mario did not talk about himself. What I learnt about him was indirect: from the things I saw around him, the people he employed, his mannerisms, his turns of phrase and the rumors I heard concerning him. In a way I felt that Mario enjoyed enveloping himself in a veil of mystery and that this was just as much a part of his character as any thing else.

As the days slipped pleasantly by I picked up more scraps of information about him. I discovered that he used to be a politician; that he was a historian and what he didn't know about Guadeloupe wasn't worth knowing. I learnt that he had connections here and there, and that he had money invested in this and that hotel. I got the impression that Mario was a power behind the scenes----that he had his finger in every pie. I was told that other hoteliers had tried to set up business in *Gosier*, but they didn't survive and that Mario was the only one who continued to prosper. I heard this and that concerning Mario and all the while I was never quite certain what was true and what was not. Mario's past remained an enigma.

Meanwhile I had seen quite a lot of Mario about the Pergola. Now and again I had spoken to him. He had shown me his ocelots and I had watched them on his shoulders licking the bald patch on his forehead. He had told me that they were not dangerous and that they were very playful, but I was wary as I had noticed that they had very sharp teeth and claws and could, of course quite playfully, scratch my eyes out. In the morning I would see Mario out in the garden in blue satin pyjamas.

"Don't touch the deer," he instructed me: "I have just put a liquid on it to get rid of the fleas"

Mario was as concerned over the welfare of his pets as a solicitous mother is over her children. However, and probably unlike many mothers, he took great care to be well informed about the needs of his animals. I was impressed by their health and cleanliness. They were well trained and I never heard any complaints about them. The guests even tolerated *Peepo's* antics with good humor. It struck me that Mario also had some sort of power to create animal lovers!

Mario also seemed to be something of a gardener: "This place used to be a marsh," he told me one evening sweeping his hand about him and indicating the area where the Pergolettes stood. "There isn't a flower, plant or tuft of grass here that I'm not responsible for. I grew everything."

So much for what I had seen of Mario's personal skills, but no less impressive were his powers as a magician. Anything you wanted and 'hey presto' Mario would see that you got it. You wanted a car, Mario found you one or lent you his; you wanted a boat, Mario would see that one was provided; you wanted to know where you should lunch when you toured the island. Mario had a restaurant at (it did not matter which part of the island you stopped Mario always had a restaurant nearby); you wanted to know where to stay in Martinique, Mario told you; you wanted to know who Père Labat was, Mario showed you his library and indicated a stack of documents; Mario, I had come to the conclusion was a travel agent, walking encyclopedia and father Christmas all rolled into one. By now I had ceased to think of my bill. I might as well enjoy myself and make the most of things, I thought.

The truth was Mario did very little directly. If a guest wanted anything he asked Guy and Guy, because he worked for Monsieur Mario, was able to command many of his powers. Guy was the go-between: he was the sorcerer apprentice; it was he who produced cars, boats, information out of a hat, so to speak, as though it was all part of some wonderful conjuring trick, but it was not to him, I felt, that the credit was due but to his boss. Guy was simply, in my opinion, a good assistant.

As for Guy himself, though I had often chatted with him, I found it difficult to get to know anything about him. He had told me a few interesting things about customs regulations, hurricanes and bread fruit, but about himself he had remained mostly silent. Even after spending a day with him I knew no more about him than if I had met him a few minutes before. His mania for speed was odd I thought. Perhaps this provided me with a clue to his character? Guy had taken us for a quick tour of the island. Quick, it should be noted, was the key note to his driving. He had driven down a country lane as though it was a German Autobahn; we had missed having several accidents by fractions of a millimeter and I had seen little of the places he had pointed out as I had been far too preoccupied with my safety.   Guy, I decided, had an inferiority complex, but that, it struck me revealed little, since most people, I thought, felt inferior about something or other, and in Guy's case I hadn't the slightest idea what it was. Guy was just as much enigma as his master.

Another person of interest who worked for Mario was his barman-waiter. This man was tall, white and heavily built. I spoke to him in French and he answered in broken English, but when I spoke to him in English he didn't answer me at all. He seemed to know neither French nor English and I got the impression that he was retarded. I wondered what nationality he was and it occurred to me that he might have been a convict and Mario was playing the role of the good Samaritan by giving him employment. I asked myself a lot of question and like a philosopher found no answers, but nevertheless continued to ask more questions.

It was only a few hours before my departure, when I was beginning to feel uncomfortable about the bill that Mario would shortly be presenting to me, that he approached me and started to answer some of the questions that I had not yet asked him but wished I had if I'd had more courage. Mario, it struck me, as a sort of last minute gesture to sugar the shock of his bill, was now going to draw up the curtain and tell me a few of his secrets

Why is it, I had wondered, that Mario didn't take more care of the

Pergola beach and why was it such a small and miserable one at that? Answer: Mario's beach, which used to be a very fine one, was destroyed by the 1956 hurricane. I was shown some photographs---before and after the disaster. Another thing I had wanted to know was where did Mario get his fine maps of Guadeloupe? The answer, I should have guessed, was quite obviously New York!

Guy, I was then told was an apprentice. He was doing a course with Mario. He had taken part of his hotelier's exams in Paris, but before he could complete his finals had to have some practical experience abroad. "He will be with me another year and this also counts towards his military service. He hopes to get a little more practical experience in Trinidad after here."

Mario then pointed to the barman-waiter. "He's from *Saint Barthelemy*. Most of the inhabitants there are white and of Nordic extraction. They have interbred and they're practically all degenerate. Many of them go to get jobs in St. Thomas. This fellow is a terrible idiot. You've got to tell him everything."

By this time I was really on tenter hooks. I was hoping, in fact almost expecting, as though it was my rightful due, that Mario would next start talking about himself. I waited patiently for him to go on, but he had decided that he had told me enough for a first visit; if I wanted to know more I must presumably return. He switched the conversation to generalities and the remaining hour before my departure passed quickly.

At last the moment I had been dreading arrived. Guy presented me with the bill. I gave it a quick look and then another more concentrated one to make quite sure that I was seeing straight: I heaved a sigh of relief: it was by no means as much as I expected. Mario leads you to believe that his bill will be colossal so that when it is only huge you are pleasantly surprised and even might go so far as to tell your friends "that really, considering everything, the Pergola is not in the least bit expensive, in fact quite cheap":

Finally I went up to Mario to say `aurevoir'. He, actor to the last for he knew several days before exactly when I was leaving, feigned complete surprise: "What. You're surely not going already!"

Martinique

There were two roads to the town and we took the shorter one first. I expected the country side to be very much like that in Guadeloupe, green and very lush with all manner of tropical vegetation, splendid beaches, rolling hills and more. But it wasn't at all the same. Martinique, though tropical appeared to have more open spaces, with the green less green. Much of the way we hugged the coast. The hills we drove over were slight, rich with grass, but with far fewer dense clusters of trees than in Guadeloupe. The sea was often visible and now and again we saw a strip of beach or a quaint little fishing village. Our driver gave us a running commentary of the scenery; and of course he didn't miss the opportunity to point out the speck of beach where Columbus had landed. The drive continued. We stopped for a meal. We stopped to look at an unusual palm---one that had two heads. We looked around the plantation where Josephine, Napoleon's wife was born and bred.

Soon we reached St. Pierre. This was the site of the old capital and the modern counterpart of Pompeii. It was here that in 1902, in less than a minute, the whole town, with its thirty thousand inhabitants was utterly destroyed. For two or three weeks prior to the disaster the nearby volcano, Mt Pelée, had been spitting out volcanic ash and clouds of it enveloped the town. The warnings were not heeded and one day (May 8 1902) there was a terrific explosion and St. Pierre ceased to exist. At the time there were eighteen ships in harbor and of these only one escaped. In the town itself there was only one survivor[1]. Fires burnt for

---

[1]

Our guide told us only about one survivor, but apparently there were two others: Pyroclastic flows completely destroyed St. Pierre, a town of 30,000 people within minutes of eruption;. The eruption left only two survivors in the direct path of the volcano (with a third reported) Louis-Auguste Cyparis survived because he was in a poorly ventilated, dungeon-like jail cell, escaped

1

three days.

We visited the little St. Pierre museum and were told the story of the one survivor. His name was Cyparis and at the time of the catastrophe had been serving a prison sentence. He had originally been put in jail for assault, but escaped as there was a carnival he particularly wanted to go to. At the end of the festivities he returned to the prison and gave himself up. The authorities, however, did not view his escape in a very charitable light and put him in a dungeon with little air and light. "Thus," said our guide, a wonderful little man of about 120, "honesty paid after all." Cyparis died in 1909, somewhat prematurely and probably due to radio activity exposure caused at the time of the eruption.

The museum consisted of one room filled with documents, photographs and fragments from the disaster. Our guide took us from picture to picture, in very much the same way a guide would in an art gallery, explaining this and that. We saw Mt Pelée as a placid pleasant green mountain; Mt Pelée enveloped in clouds of grey ash and finally as a roaring volcano spitting lava a 1,000 feet into the air. The guide took us to the ruins of the church, fort and theater. On the floor and in display cases we saw chunks of lava, scorched rock, twisted iron, melted beer bottles, crumpled cooking utensils and a great number of other relics, distorted and scorched..

After a quick look round the new St. Pierre, a glimpse of a few ruins, a snap shot or two, we returned to Fort de France. This time we took the longer interior route. We climbed rapidly out of St. Pierre and soon we had a splendid view of Mt Pelée. What we saw was the placid pleasant green mountain of that first picture our guide had shown us. It was difficult to imagine this mountain as an angry volcano and even when I tried to visualize the other pictures I had seen it was always the one of the placid pleasant green one that superimposed itself on my imagination. Presently the countryside became greener. Trees were

---

with severe burns." (Wikipedia encyclopdia)

2

more numerous, but never so dense or lush as in Guadeloupe.

We saw the usual island products: oranges, lemons, paw-paws, coffee, beans, guavas, breadfruit, mangoes. Everything had a symmetry about it which somehow destroyed that wild beauty I had appreciated so much in Guadeloupe. We stopped a moment and our driver went and broke a few pieces of bark off a nearby tree. "Cinnamon,"he said and gave us a sniff. We drove on.

A mongoose darted across the road and this prompted the driver to tell us how they first came to the island. The story seemed feasible, but I don't vouch for its veracity. He said that snakes, the terrible Fer-de-lance, were imported into the island by planters to prevent their slaves from escaping. When slavery was abolished the snakes had to be got rid of; and so mongooses were brought to the island. The driver laughed: "Now we've got the Fer-de-lance and the mongoose,"

3

Anything Can Happen In Trinidad

Speaking as a tourist I find it difficult to tell whether Trinidadians hate tourists more than tourists hate Trinidadians. For my part, since I cannot be two things at once, I can only express the view-point of the tourist.

"When are you leaving?" welcomed the immigration officer a few moments after we had arrived.

"I'm not quite sure. If possible I should like permission to stay four months."

After a few more peremptory questions the official generously allowed me to stay in the Colony three days. "If you go to the Immigration Authorities tomorrow they'll extend your permission to stay here," he said.

Next I found myself speeding down a well surfaced bituminous road. Fortunately it was night and I couldn't appreciate how dangerously fast we were going, though I had a shrewd suspicion we were well above the speed limit.

There was a lot of traffic. I got the impression I was in the Monte Carlo rally. Nobody dipped their lights. On one or two occasions I nearly witnessed an accident. The taxi driver would laugh: "Anything can happen in Trinidad," he would cry and with this comforting philosophy put his foot hard down on the accelerator.

It was not until I'd been in Trinidad a few days that I appreciated the wisdom of that taxi driver. Here was this man, presumably little educated, who had, in one short phrase, summed up probably everything there was to say about Trinidad. He had done what the philosopher strives to do all his life: He had found truth. "Anything can happen in Trinidad" was true.

My first experience of this was that I was solemnly warned not to go out at night. "It's dangerous explained my informer and went on to say that there were a lot of murders in Trinidad. People got cut up and robbed for a penny, and that anything could happen in Trinidad.

A few days later I was having an argument on crime prevention with a Trinidadian. I was arguing against capital punishment. I said I didn't see what good it did since most murders were spontaneous, committed on impulse.

He smiled knowingly: "People usually know when there's going to be a spontaneous murder. You see the culprit will be sharpening his - cutlass all the previous night."

This good gentleman then went on to tell me that prisons in Trinidad were like good hotels. I got the impression that it was a privilege to get into one. He made me feel very foolish at what I was paying at my guest house when I could have been so delightfully accommodated free. He also assured that the cat-of-nine-tails wasn't used enough and nowadays, even when it was used, was like a pleasant caress.

This gentleman was not alone, however, in his charitableness to his fellow islanders. "You can't possibly over estimate the intelligence of the average Trinidadian," a man in a fairly prominent position assured me. Then again an official didn't seem to have a high regard for politicians. When you've voted in Trinidad you have to dip your finger in a red stain, so that it can be seen that you've voted and won't vote twice. One man objected to putting his finger in the offensive liquid: "This is the last time I'll vote," he protested.

The official laughed: "It's probably the last opportunity you'll get to vote".

And so gradually, from these odd scraps of information a picture of Trinidad began to form itself in my mind. I had been told that there were 52 murders in the colony last year; that there were 68 cinemas on the island, (this I find hard to believe, but then anything is possible in Trinidad) and that as soon as one Carnival was over Trinidadians started preparing for the next.

All this information, carefully imparted to me by long standing Trinidadians, led me to the conclusion that the average Trinidadian had the twenty four hours of his day well mapped out. In the morning he prepared for Carnival; in the afternoon and evening he went to the pictures and at night he sharpened his cutlass!

So much for indirect impressions. Let we now relate a few personal experiences. The first concerns a kind gentleman who promised to drive me round the island. "I'll pick you up at 6:30 Sunday morning at your guest house," he said.

I hate getting up early, but on this occasion made a special effort. By some miracle I was ready on time. It was a lovely day and I was looking forward to the drive. I waited.

After an hour of waiting I went in and had breakfast. The kind gentleman never came and I have not seen or heard from him since. I dismissed the incident from my mind: "Anything can happen in Trinidad," I consoled myself.

A few days later another Trinidadian played the same trick on me. This fellow, however, was not so brutal as to make me get up at the crack of down. "I'll ring you first," he promised. I remained in Trinidad two more weeks, but never heard from him.

The same sort of thing happens when I go into a shop here. No sooner have I set foot in a store than the attendant flees. I have almost to go down on bended knee to get service. The only exception to this rule being when I go into a book shop. There the service is instantaneous. (Of course in a book shop I hate being served for I haven't the slightest intention of buying anything and only want to browse!)

What with one thing and another it seemed to me that Trinidadians were not going about things the right way if they wanted to attract tourists. "Surely you want visitors to like this island and come and spend money in it," I said to a Trinidadian one day.

He gave me a surprised look and then told me that Trinidadians were no more keen to have tourists to the colony than the fer-de-lance.

"Why is that?" I asked somewhat bewildered.

"Because we don't want our character spoilt," he answered calmly. "You see Trinidad floats on oil."

In an instant I understood everything. It was obvious now why I had been so warmly welcomed at the airport; it was clear why the taxi driver had tried to frighten me out of my wits; it was perfectly understandable why the two kind gentlemen had left me in the lurch and why shop attendants had been so reluctant to serve me. I, and the likes of me, were not wanted. I was that horrible monster---a tourist.

Once I had gained this insight I began to see Trinidad with different eyes. I saw fine buildings, an agricultural college, good roads, how people of many races mixed and a hundred and one little things that had previously escaped my attention. I realized that anything can happen in Trinidad!

Ms Stollmeyer's Guest House

Whatever I have said about Trinidad so far simply does not apply to the Guest House[1] I was in. This was a tall dirty white wooden structure that overlooked the Savannah. It looked about a hundred years old and everything about it was antiquated: the large rooms, the high ceilings, the wooden beams, the steep staircase and on it goes. The atmosphere however was friendly and I felt at home. Miss Stollmeyer's Guest House was not so much exemplary as a century out of date.

Lunch and dinner were the big events of the day. We had our meals on the verandah at one long table with, at one end, the redoubtable Miss Stollmeyer presiding. She was a woman of great bulk, great charm and immense sense of humor. She was, and referred to herself as such: *The Battle Axe*, adding that I could call her that if I wanted. I never did, however, for I had a shrewd suspicion she was as tough as a battle axe. Allowing us (all visitors were included) to call her names was not the limit of her solicitousness. Miss Stollmeyer also lavished immense concern over the gastronomical interests of her guests. The food was simply disgusting, especially the meat, but nevertheless she was all the time asking us whether we liked it, did we want more, was Mr so and so satisfied with the lamb chop, etc etc. When we refused second helpings she would press us in her concerned way: "You can only die once you know." I never had the courage to tell her that what she said was not true: that since I had been at her table I had died a score of times. Instead, now and again, I tried to get a little of my own back: "Why don't you have a second helping Miss Stollmeyer? It's so good." She would look at me forgivingly, her eyes twinkling, as though to say she wasn't born yesterday: "When you're as young as I am you've got to look after your figure," she would reply.

Eventually I became one of the honored guests and sat on Miss

---

[1] The price of a room in a Guest House is for board and lodge---usually breakfast and dinner, though in some cases lunch is also provided.

Stollmeyer's right. From this vantage point I was able to learn something about her. She belonged to a very wealthy and old Trinidadian family, which had become considerably impoverished and was not far from extinction. In its heyday it had owned half the island and the name of Stollmeyer was a byword for power, prestige and respectability. Years before she had traveled extensively in Western Europe and the islands and she never ceased to tell me that traveling was a wonderful (the best) education. At present she was a Spiritualist. She attacked Christianity with the fervor of a Crusade, saying that Catholics were hypocrites, priests rogues and the Pope the devil; that since the instigation of Christianity there had never been so much wickedness. She fed me with spiritualistic literature to reenforce her views, but I can vouch that she could have done all the work herself, for there was nothing wrong with her vocal chords.

On the other side of Miss Stollmeyer and opposite me sat Mary. She was a permanent resident, quiet, plump and Catholic ---a woman who believed in her religion, but probably never thought about it. Everybody liked her, especially the cats. For these she would scrounge the remains from other peoples' plates (always considerable) and then with infinite care remove bones, splinters and I suppose other things cats do not like and chop everything up and arrange it into neat equal little piles for each animal..

So much for food and cats. Outside this field Mary was, I regret to say, somewhat limited. Her small talk betokened a person with little education and no great love of music or literature. Needless to say then, although we enjoyed her company, we never expected her to make a brilliant remark or contribute to our knowledge. It was quite a surprise then, when one day she did precisely that. We were discussing the etymology of certain words and now Mary, without any prompting from us, volunteered the suggestion that the word "Lawyer" originated from "Liar". This was a revelation which received its proper due by a moment of silence. It was spoilt however by Mary, no doubt troubled by the fact that she was not used to being the center of attention, quickly returned to her normal self by telling us something we, of course, all knew:"All lawyers are liars," she said, as though in self-defense.

The only other person at our table who was not just a guest of very short duration was Mr O. He sat a few places down from Mary and judging by his appearance (thin, sallow, long faced) looked as though he would shortly be executed. Saturnine perhaps describes him best. I don't really know what a manic depressive looks like, but I believe he would have qualified as a good prototype. He attended meals with obsessional punctuality, but never opened his mouth, other than to stuff it with food. If he wanted anything he pointed; if Miss Stollmeyer asked him if everything was all right, he nodded; if he did not want something, he shook his head. As soon as he had finished eating he left the table. Miss Stollmeyer one day surreptitiously whispered in my ear that he and Mary should marry. I was not cruel enough to wish her that! For my part I was rather nervous eating at the same table as him, for I had a persistent premonition he would suddenly rise and in front of us all give us a spectacular demonstration of Harakiri.

The only other person in the guest house who was a permanent resident, but did not have meals with us was Mrs A. ("I prefer my own company," she would say.) She was a skinny little woman in her sixties, who was of Scottish descent (very proud of it too), but had lived in Trinidad for very many years. Her room was on the landing in the front part of the Guest House and it was always in the most frightful mess. There were books, magazines, papers, cases, bags, baskets, materials and knickknacks of every conceivable description scattered about the place. From this mess Mrs A. would now and again emerge. Usually she timed this admirably to coincide with my tip-toeing past her door, going up or down stairs that is. "Ah!" she would exclaim in her exquisite Scottish accent and then tag on the suitable greeting for that particular time of day. If I could manage it I made good my escape, but sometimes I was caught and was forced to listen. On these occasions Mrs A. would tell me the story of her life, difficulties with Miss Stollmeyer, money and lawyer problems; and all this interspersed, gratuitously so to speak, with gems of her precious wisdom. Everybody thought Mrs A. quite mad, but I found her (in small doses) very entertaining and deliciously funny.

Now and again I would provoke her. One day we were discussing cards and she said she played bridge.

"What system do you use?" I asked maliciously, convinced she used none.

She gave me a hard look. "My system," she replied, "I bid the cards you know."

Another time I said that as soon as a Scot reached the age of reason he left Scotland. There were more Scottish people out of country than in it.

"That's only because we're wanted for all the better jobs all over the world," she smiled.

On yet another occasion I was telling Mrs A. I was frightened of green dragons. "Are you frightened of green dragons Mrs A.?" I asked.

She laughed. "Me. I'm frightened of nothing, except certain things that I do not want to talk about."

Soon and back at the Guest House some newcomers arrived. The Federal Parliament would shortly be opening and MPs from all the other British islands began to pour into Port of Spain, the provisional capital of the Federation. At Stollmeyer's Guest House we had three: two from Jamaica and one from Barbados. A boxer also joined our group about this time, but I do not think he had anything to do with the Federation unless he was body-guard for one of the members of Parliament. In this capacity, however, I do not think his services were required.

Meal times now became more animated. Most of the time I was caught between an incessant flow of dishes: the meat, gravy, vegetables, cat food, etc. There were so many people at the table that Mr 0. had almost crawled beneath it, for not only did he not talk, but he was hardly visible. Next to me however, far from invisible, sat Mr P, one of the Jamaican MPs. He was a tall black man, extraordinary good looking and with an immense amount of charm. He had been to Oxford where he had collected not only blues, but also an impeccable Oxford accent. In his beautifully modulated voice he was forever flattering Miss Stollmeyer on the excellence of her cuisine: "This is really delicious Miss Stollmeyer;", "Very good thank you Miss Stollmeyer," "Just perfect Miss Stollmeyer" And so he went on. I could not help noticing however that he had most of his meals out. Mr P. was the perfect diplomat and as a politician exemplary. Not only did he look and act the part, but he made the right noises which, as any student of politics knows, is far more important than making sense. His hobbies were playing the piano, travelling, giving parties and associating with celebrities. The least of his interests was politics.

The other two politicians were less flamboyant and from them I was able to learn a little about the planned Federation. They explained that, for the moment they were in the blue print stage: that, although they had achieved certain cultural exchanges, their main problems were the distribution of seats in Parliament, customs barriers and free migration. Jamaica was by far the wealthiest of the islands; and there was fear that, on the one hand, it would, by virtue of its power, exercise too much control over the other islands and, on the other hand, that it (Jamaica} would be drained of its wealth by the rest of the group. For it to withdraw from the Federation however would have inevitably meant its collapse, for the other islands were not strong enough to go it alone. A certain amount of canvassing had been done to draw British Guiana (BG as it is often called) into the Federation with a view to redressing the distribution of power, but this (to date) had proved unsuccessful. British Guiana was a country with immense potential, not an island and with problems entirely different to those of the other British Caribbean territories. The powers that be decided, for the time being, to do nothing, but simply watch the Federal experiment unfold..

To add to these difficulties the islands' peoples were by no means homogenous. Religion and language were common denominators but race, color and historical background differed considerably. Of these variegations race was undoubtedly the most important. Throughout the islands White and Black mixed with varying degrees of assimilation, but never completely. In Trinidad the position was further aggravated by a large East Indian population as well as a large Chinese minority[2]. Here, I discovered soon after my arrival, tension was at its worst. The atmosphere was volcanic with every racial group hating every other. In this atmosphere it was impossible, for each island, to be proportionately represented. For instance, if British Guiana joined the Federation the Indians would be disproportionately represented: something quite unacceptable to the Blacks.

Armed with these smatterings of knowledge I gladly accepted an invitation by the M.P.s to go to one of their sessions. They were very friendly and gave me a proper Cook's tour of Federal House: the provisional building used for their meetings The object of Federation was that eventually the British Caribbean territories would achieve Dominion Status. After a while they took me to the public gallery and left me to watch. The House soon filled up and business began. Accents varied considerably and I often had difficulty understanding what was going on. Nevertheless, I did get the impression that the atmosphere was democratic and that the standard of debate was no worse (which is not saying much) than in the House of Commons.

In due course I was rejoined by the MPs who had brought me and we went and had tea. I was introduced to a score of members, including the Federal Prime Minister, the leader of the opposition and the speaker. I got the opportunity to speak to several Trinidadian MPs and they gave me an interesting slant on the internal situation. An East Indian began with a long account of the grimy politics on his island. He said that the

---

[2] The approximate population distribution in Trinidad at the time (1960) was as follows: Negroes 55%; Indians 35%; Chinese 5% and Whites 5%.

Whites had the money, then the Indians, followed by the Chinese; the Blacks had the political power. The Prime Minister, Williams, he went on to say, was quite disreputable. He had a wife and children in the States, but did nothing for them and there had been some scandal a little later when he had remarried a Chinese girl without first divorcing his wife in America. At the last general election he had made a specific issue of race; and jobs were always jobs for the boys. Every election, he continued, was fraught with violence and Williams did nothing to discourage it. As for the Governor he was a "weed"; but his term of office was very nearly at an end and the new Governor promised to be better.

Later, when I had met both Indian and Negro[3] Trinidadians I discovered not so much that their stories differed, but that the role they played in them were reversed. When an Indian was speaking he was the protagonist and the Black the villain: it was the Blacks who were corrupt, racially conscious, addicted to violence and the cause of all the trouble on the island. On the other hand, when I was speaking to a Black I got the impression that the Indians were clannish, dishonest, always fighting to spread their power and the cause of much evil on the island. About their Prime Minister they remained completely silent. The only conclusion I came to about politics in Trinidad was that they were not very nice. But then perhaps they are not many places where they are?

The company at Stollmeyer's Guest House was anything but dull and since 'Anything can happen in Trinidad' I would not be in the least bit surprised if the place was now a lunatic asylum.

---

[3] When this was written *Negro* was the word used for Blacks. It was also, at the time the term used by the islanders themselves.

From Trinidad to Brazil

I was going round the world. I had very little money and would be forced to travel cheap or earn something as I went along. I was in Trinidad on my way to South America, where I knew I was unlikely to find work. I had air travel vouchers for as far as Santiago, Chile. It struck me if I could somehow use them economically it would be a savings. After some research I discovered that a sea trip to Belem[1] and an internal flight to Rio would reduce my travel expenses by more than two thirds. Fine, I thought, but hesitated for I do not like sea travel. The smell of ships makes me nauseous. I get easily sea sick. I don't like the confinement. Pills don't help either. Most of the time I lie on my bunk feeling sorry for myself. Once, I had traveled from Southampton to New York on the Queen Mary. The accommodation, the food, entertainment, the ship's stabilizers, had all been A1. Yet, notwithstanding a relatively calm sea, I had been quite sick. There would be none of the Queen Mary's comforts on a cargo boat. What's more I would have to share a cabin, something I didn't relish. The agent in Port of Spain assured me there were only two births per cabin and that the journey took only four days. The savings, I decided, would be worth the inconvenience.

* * * * *

No visas had been required so far on my trip. Now I would need one to get into Brazil. I went to the local consulate. A dapper young official, after not acknowledging me for an appropriate number of minutes, asked what I wanted. I told him and he handed me a sheet of paper. The stipulations were as follows:

---

[1] Belem is in northern Brazil at the mouth of the Amazon and is two degrees above the equator, but as Brazil is in the southern hemisphere it too is considered part of that hemisphere.

- *Forms completed in quadruplet*
- *4 photographs with a white background*
- *Guarantee of £100.*
- *Return ticket*
- *Smallpox vaccination*
- *Medical examination*
- *Fee of B.W.I.[2] $3.60* (about U.S. $3 at the time)

"What do you mean photographs, white background?" I asked.

"The picture must be taken against a white background."

"I have photographs with a grey background.."

"That won't do"

"You surely don't expect me to have a new set of photographs made just because you want a white background? Why, even the photograph in my passport has a grey background."

"It would be unfair to make an exception in your case."

"Don't you want tourists in Brazil? You ask your consul if he can make an exception in my case?"

He nodded. "I shall ask him."

We passed on to the next item.

"Will travel vouchers do instead of a return ticket?"

"What are travel vouchers?"

I explained.

"I shall have to ask the consul."

"Who pays for the medical examination?" I pursued.

"You do."

I knew I wouldn't get away with this one, but I was feeling argumentative and decided to press on: "But it's expensive. I'm a student. I can't afford a medical examination. I assure you I'm in excellent health."

---

[2] British West Indies dollars

"The medical examination is not expensive and we can recommend a doctor."

"Where is he?"

"Downstairs."

"When can I see him? Do I have to make an appointment?"

"No. You can go to him when you like. When you bring back the forms you will be able to see him then."

A week later I was again facing the dapper young man.

"Will my photographs do?" I asked

"In your case the consul has decided to make an exception."

I thawed a little. "Thank him very much."

There was a pause while he examined my forms.

"Did you ask about the travel vouchers?"

"In your case the consul has decided to make an exception."

"Thank you very much." And I asked him if he wanted to see them.

"That will not be necessary."

"Do you want to see my £100?"

"That will not be necessary." He leant over confidentially. "When you were here last there was another man in the room. It wouldn't have been fair to show you were a special case."

I smiled, gushed, thanked him profusely. I had not seen anybody in the room on my previous visit.

"If you go downstairs Doctor Hill will see you."

After more thanks I went to find Doctor Hill.

I was less than a minute in the waiting room. Then I was ushered into the doctor's study. He did not ask me to sit down, but enquired about the nature of my visit. I told him.

"How do you feel?" he asked.

"Fine," I answered. .

He took out a piece of paper from a drawer and scribbled something on it, stamped it and gave it to me. "That will be one dollar

163

please."

*   *   *   *   *

I had managed to convert part of my travel vouchers for the sea trip. I was ready to go. The first piece of bad news came about a week later. The agent informed me that our departure had been postponed three days and that now we would not be going direct to Belem but via La Guiara, a port off Caracas in Venezuela. The boat would be docked there for a couple of days to unload cargo. The trip would be extended to eight days. The agent had warned me that when traveling rough and cheap anything was possible. The only guarantee was the final destination.

I had arranged my finances so that I would have just enough money to pay the taxi to the dock. Another phone call from the agent changed all that. I was now informed that there was a further delay of twenty four hours. Fortunately, the landlady at my Guest House was a kind and generous soul. "Be my guest," she said when I told her my predicament. I made vague promises to advertise her lodgings in the four corners of the globe.

*   *   *   *   *

The place was deserted. No officials. No passengers. No crew. I began to panic. Had I got the right day? Was I in the right place? Did I misunderstand the agent? A few tugs and fishing boats were in dock as well as one larger ship, flying a Panamanian flag. Was that it, I wondered? I waited. I hung around for about hour, then a short, skinny, dark young woman struggling with a couple of bags and a suitcase appeared. She too was to make the trip. We reassured each other that we were on time and had not missed the boat.

As soon as I saw him I knew I would be sharing my cabin with him. He was a medium-sized man, middle-height, middle-aged, bald, with glasses, deaf aid and carrying a suit case and haversack. His clothes were light, tattered and grubby. He looked as though he had just walked across the Sahara desert and was now going to trudge through the Brazilian jungle Even before he spoke I knew he was English. The Public School mold was written all over him: the clean-cut features, a certain ruggedness accompanied by reserve and pride, an empire builder from a bye-gone age.

All the while I was chatting with the dark girl. Then very gingery he approached us.

"Do you know what time the boat leaves?" he asked.

His voice startled me. It was very high pitched, squeaky, like a long playing record run at the wrong speed. Here's a rum bird, I said to myself. Aloud, and I bellowed, for now there was a lot of commotion. I told him I hadn't a clue: that probably the boat had already sailed. Politely he pointed out that it was hardly likely. He then introduced himself as William ("call me Bill," he said,) and told us he was something of a globe trotter and had just come from Australia where he had spent a couple of years. I sensed he might be useful to me, and immediately began bombarding him with questions. He said everything I didn't want to hear. South America was very expensive. Peru was particularly so. I wouldn't be able to get a job in any of these countries because of language and permit requirements. If I wanted work I must go to Australia. It was tough there, but I'd be able to get a job all right.

"How about Hong-Kong?"

"There's probably nothing you can do that a Cantonese can't do. And anyway they're prepared to work for a pittance whereas you probably aren't."

"What about talks on the radio?" I asked.

"Yes," he admitted that was a possibility and then and went on to say that when he was there he met an eccentric old lady who used to give travel talks. She talked nonsense apparently. Perhaps I could do the same?

He then switched to talking about India. It was very cheap, he said.

If I lived like a native and carried my bed around with me I could live on two or three shillings a day. Or if I wanted to be even more frugal I could put up at a Dharamshales. This, he explained, was a Jain temple and was free, anyway for the first three days. "But your best bet is Australia." He returned to his original recommendation, as though mentioning anything else was a waste of time.

Can you get there from Santiago in Chile? I was about to ask him when we were cut short by an unpleasant rumor that now reached us. News was spreading that a telegram had been received from La Guiara saying there was no docking space there. We would have to go to Puerto Cabello, a port some 200 miles further up the Venezuelan coast. I didn't like that at all. La Guiara is a short distance from Caracas and I had a cousin living there and wanted to visit with her. Besides, I thought, and I threw William an angry glance, it would probably mean two more nights with that slob. As I was thinking this I realized he was looking at me a bit oddly and it struck me that he might be having similar misgivings about me.

A little crowd had gathered a few yards away from us. We drifted towards it and lingered in an attempt to pick up a few scraps of information. Some half dozen Venezuelans were arguing frantically. They were bombarding the unfortunate agent representative with gesticulations and questions. They wanted to know who was going to pay for the journey from Puerto Cabello to Caracas. One thing was certain, they wouldn't. They went on and on. The travel clerk suffered in silence.

This went on for about fifteen minutes, then somebody from the ship turned up and said a telegram had been sent to the company's head office in London. There would be no change in the ship's itinerary without authorization from London. We would proceed to La Guiara as arranged.[3]

"When do we sail?" somebody asked.

The reply was unexpected: "This afternoon."

A few minutes later I was boarding. The usual smells greeted me: rope, oil, garbage, stale air, cabbage—all sort of intertwined and with other indeterminate but objectionable odors. I found my cabin and dumped my things in it. Then, I had a look around. The ship looked much the same as the few others I had been on. First class space was about five times greater than that of tourist class for probably about a fifth of the passengers. It was impossible to find a quiet spot on the tourist deck. Rowdy Portuguese children were everywhere and besides their parents had grabbed all the deck chairs and seats. I returned to the cabin.

My things were still the only ones there. I began to hope that I'd have the cabin to myself. After all if nobody had turned up by now there was reason to suppose I'd be on my own. I took a few things out of my valise and then, fully resolved to find a quiet spot on the first class deck, left the cabin. As I was doing so I bumped into William.

"Do you know where cabin number 8 is?" he asked in his polite shrill voice.

My heart fell. "This is it," I replied tonelessly.

I sat on a bunk as he unpacked. Might as well make the most of him, I thought. I asked him if it was possible to go from Valparaiso, Chile to Australia. He didn't hear me the first time, so I shrieked the question again.

He shook his head. "There's no way of crossing the Pacific from the west coast of South America. You have to go to Panama first. Even then it's very difficult to find a passage and you might have to wait months."

"Is it expensive," I shouted.

---

[3] We ended up going to Puerto Cabello

"Very. The cheapest line is the French one. If you're lucky you'll be able to get a place in the hold for a little over £100."

"And if I go to Australia from Panama is it possible to stop-over at some of the Pacific Islands?"

"No. The shipping companies do not allow you to break your journey. You have to go to Australia or Fiji if you want to go to the Pacific islands and then the only way to get to most of them is by air."

At that moment the lunch gong went. This gave me the opportunity to slip away. William's gloomy replies depressed me. In the dining room I seated myself next to the Trinidadian girl and began scrutinizing the menu.

"May I join you?"

It was Bill and he asked the question like you say how-do-you-do, that is to say without the slightest interest to what the reply would be. I passed him the menu. It struck me as foolish to bear him any grudge. After all he had done me no harm and it wasn't his fault we were sharing the same cabin. I resolved to pick his brains further.

"If I somehow managed to stop off at one of the Pacific islands what chance would I have of finding work?"

"None. None at all. There's nothing on them. They're even less developed than those in the West Indies, the ones you've recently been to."

"You think Australia's my best bet then?"

He nodded. "You'll be able to manage there. But it's tough. For instance, there are no porters at the stations. It's foolish to have more luggage than you can carry." Then he told us about a little old lady who couldn't find a porter and had to return from where she came from.

"How did she get her luggage on the train in the first place?" I shot back.

"A friend probably took her to the station and carried it for her."

If he had noticed a note of triumph in my riposte he didn't show it. He continued: work possibilities in New Zealand were good, he said. The problem there wasn't finding a job, but keeping it. New Zealanders apparently didn't like foreigners. If a stranger went to work with them they said nothing, but made you feel so uncomfortable that in the end you wanted to leave.

"What country have you liked the most?" asked the Trinidadian girl.

Bill cocked his deaf aid. The question was repeated. There was a pause, then he flashed a fine row of crooked teeth: "I like them all the same," he said.

*   *   *   *   *

It was late afternoon when we set sail. The sky was perfectly blue and the sea a mirror of oil. I stood on the deck gazing out at the last of the small islands bordering on Trinidad.. Next to me was Bill. "Isn't it hot!" he moaned.

Birds swooped low over the water, never quite touching it and I was impressed by their large wing span and majesty. I pretended not to hear him.

*   *   *   *   *

The journey to Puerto Cabello was without incident. (Though it had not been rough, I had spent much of my time on my bunk.) Lining the dock, awaiting our arrival, were six huge refrigerator vans with men scurrying to and fro, clad in white from head to toe as though ready for a polar expedition. We were carrying 300 tons of Irish beef and this was now to be loaded on the vans and taken to Caracas. Apparently the work would go on non-stop for 48 hours. I watched for a while then went in to dinner.

Next day I traipsed around Puerto Cabello with Bill. It was not much of a place, though it looked clean and prosperous. At the time (1961) Caracas was reputed to be the most expensive city in the world and certainly there was a spillover of high prices to the surrounding areas. Puerto Cabello remains the only place I have ever been to where American dollars were not acceptable currency. The shop attendant wouldn't even deign to touch the twenty dollar bill I offered her. "I don't want that," she said. "In Venezuela we accept only Bolivars." She emphasized `Bolivars' as though she was talking about something sacred.

My excursions into Venezuelan prices made me wonder what the beef we were carrying would sell for in the local markets. Ireland, so I was told, had priced its meat at 10/- a pound. This included delivery to a Venezuelan port. However, because we had switched to Puerto Cabello a whole set of new arrangements had had to be made. These involved carrying the beef in refrigerator vans to the local airport, then to Caracas's airport (not far from La Guiara) where it would be collected by the original assignment of refrigerated vans scheduled to distribute it throughout the capital. The meat would sell retail for between 12/6 and 14/- per pound. ($1.80 to $2.00 at the time.) However, because the trip had been extended the suppliers in Ireland had panicked and ordered the meat to be frozen while still on the ocean. It was to be sold as "chilled beef", but I have little doubt that by the time it got to the consumer it would be de-frozen and re-frozed chilled meat.

*   *   *   *   *

It is appropriate to say more about Bill. I spent a good deal of time with him, not only at meals, wandering around Porto Cabello, in the cabin but also (when I was feeling well enough) on deck and in the lounges. Bill had been to a Grammar School, a Northern University and was by profession a bacteriologist. He had had several stints of three year contracts, but as he liked traveling did not stay long in any one place. Work, for him was no more than a means to an end. He spoke several languages badly and though he could always make himself understood preferred visiting the English speaking countries, for it was easier to find work in them. He had never married. He said nothing about a sex life. When he spoke about women it was as though they had been neutered. He didn't know when he was going to retire or where, but when he did he would take up gardening. He had little respect for politicians and even less for academics, who, he claimed, achieved their university status mainly through political manoeuver and intrigue. Bill was a nice man, sensitive, thoughtful, always courteous. However, there was something odd about him. Perhaps his extensive traveling and solitariness had something to do with it, I don't know. His voice was not the only thing that was peculiar. He also had a nervous twitch, which took the form of screwing up his nose and face very unexpectedly so that you got the impression that he had just received an electric shock. Then, he would use the palms of both hands, like an optometrist, to adjust the arms of his thin black rimmed spectacles which had tipped to one side.

But Bill was also a reservoir of stories. I recount a few that I recall. We were talking about milk. I don't remember exactly why. I think it was at dinner and the Trinidadian girl or me asked how long it kept under refrigeration. He answered promptly like the competent bacteriologist I took him to be. I regret to say that I do not remember his reply, but only the sequel. Refrigeration, he said, was an old fashioned way of preserving milk. A new machine had been invented, which made a whistling sound over the milk. This so shook up the germs that they found it impossible to stay, thus the milk could be preserved indefinitely.

We were impressed.

"Anyway," he continued: "very shortly it won't be necessary to store milk at all. Another machine has been invented which makes it out of garbage. All you have to do is feed trash into one end of the machine and a white milky substance comes out of the other. They say it's as good as milk!"

Another of his stories concerned a Swiss fellow who migrated to Brazil in the thirties with only £5 in his pocket. Naturally, the money did not last long and he soon found himself stranded. He appealed to his consulate, but was told that `Le Ministre' did not see people like him. The Swiss, however, was persistent. He returned again and again to the Consulate until, in the end, the Minister was so impressed by his tenacity that he agreed to see him.

"`I want to give you a word of advice,' began the Consul as soon as his compatriot was ushered into his presence and before the poor fellow had time to say a word. `Don't drink and have nothing to do with women and you'll be all right.' He then proceeded to help him"

We waited for him to go on..

Silence.

"What happened then?" I asked eventually.

He twitched, adjusted his spectacles and seemed quite put out, as though I had asked him a very personal question. Then, it struck me that the look, as though he was ill at ease, was an act, a ploy to keep us on tenterhooks. I was expecting some sort of stinging O' Henry twist.

"I don't know," he replied when he had collected himself. "I never heard the end of the story."

Then, as though he needed to vindicate himself after letting us down, hurried on with another yarn. The tale concerned an Italian soldier in the Western Desert who believed he had swallowed a snake. He was examined by one of the ward doctors who assured him he was perfectly well. The soldier was adamant. He insisted that if he wasn't operated on very soon he would die. The doctor humored him for a while by giving him pills. These did no good and the patient got worse. The doctor began to have doubts about his diagnosis. He examined the soldier more thoroughly, had him X-rayed and sent him to see other physicians. The prognostications were always the same: there was nothing wrong with him. Meanwhile, the soldier's health deteriorated. Soon he was at death's door and the doctor did what, under the circumstances, can only be described as his duty. He operated.

"And was there a snake?" the Trinidadian girl asked.

Bill smiled. "I don't know," he replied. "You see the doctor never bothered to find out. He just cut him open and sewed him straight up again."

"And then what?" I asked cautiously. I wanted to be prepared for another anticlimax.

Bill squeaked with relish. "He recovered immediately."

"What," I said a little startled. "Without any cure or anything?"

"Well not exactly." He paused and then went on: "You see the doctor did have a good deal of trouble finding a snake to show him."

*   *   *   *   *

We arrived in Belem on December 21st, exactly one day before the official commencement of winter in the northern hemisphere. As soon as we docked twelve men, dark, with black moustaches, wearing red arm bands, presumably a symbol of their authority and Brazilian red tape, came aboard. We were instructed to go up to the First Class lounge, where our documents would be checked by Immigration. Armed with my passport, vaccination and medical certificates as well as a couple of disembarkation cards, I joined a long line of passengers.

The twelve men were at work. There were three tables with four men at each. This was Brazil's defense against an alien invasion.

Eventually I got to the beginning of the line. This was table one. Here a man ticked off my name on a sheet of paper. The second took my disembarkation card, while the third stamped my vaccination certificate. Then I was asked to move on to table two. My name was again ticked off, my passport stamped (in the center of the page, so that it could not be used for any other visa) and the third man added his signature with a flourish across the stamp that had just been made by his colleague. At the third table the ritual was not very different from the previous one. My name was ticked off, my passport was again stamped, but this time dated by the third Immigration officer, who smiled at me and announced: "E tudo" (that is all). The fourth man's job at each table, it seemed to me, was to make sure his co-workers were well supplied with coffee and other refreshments. This formality lasted nearly two hours, but if I imagined that was the end of it I a surprise in store for me.

Next item on the agenda was customs.

When we were through with immigration we were allowed to disembark. Of course our passports were again checked at the gangway. I let myself be dragged along by the crowd to where, I hoped, to recover my baggage. My porter had said he would meet me at customs. It was sweltering hot. There were no signs. People were irritable and confused. Nobody seemed to know where to go or what to do. Questions were asked, but there were no officials around and it was a case of the blind leading the blind. Eventually I did find the customs shed. There was a problem getting into it, however, for it was enormous with only a very small entrance, which you had to first find and then crush your way through. Luggage, of every size, color and shape, was stacked, with no apparent logic, in little heaps all across the floor. I kept an eye out for my porter, but as he was not wearing a uniform he was indistinguishable from passengers.

I am not a particularly patient person, but realized that if I wanted to avoid high blood pressure, a stroke or worse, I would have to keep my calm. I hung around and eventually my porter found me. The next problem was to get my baggage cleared. This procedure I can only describe as diabolical. The scheme was a credit to Brazilian ingenuity. The closest parallel I can find to it is to say it resembled, though much more complicated, the game of HUNT-THE-THIMBLE[4]. The first thing you had to do was to find one of two men (and there were no more) who were giving out customs declaration forms. They were distinguishable by virtue of being the only persons with the forms.

After a good deal of wandering and without the advantages of being told "hot" or "cold" I did find a throng of people screaming and waving their arms, hustling and pushing. I joined the battle and soon I was struggling to grab a form from the official at the epicenter. Of course it wasn't that simple. Each form had a name on it and I would have to find mine. As things turned out this particular official didn't have it. I wandered off in search of the other one. In due course I found him and,

---

[4] The game consists of hiding a thimble and being told 'getting hotter' 'getting colder' respectively as you got nearer or further from the thimble.

only after a few bruises, got my form. As things turned out, it should have been completed aboard the ship. I realized it made more sense to get my own particular one back if, as required, I had filled it up earlier. Maybe a crucial announcement had escaped me or perhaps it had only been in Portuguese? Anyway, my next task was to persuade, without speaking the language, the official to inspect my baggage. This took some time, though the actual clearance lasted less than a minute. I was asked one question, then quick chalk marks were scribbled on my luggage. Customs was over. It had lasted a little more than three hours.

In the street I bumped straight into Bill. We had finished formalities more or less at the same time, though, because of their nature, we had had to go our separate ways. He now informed me with his usual optimistic squeak that it would be impossible to find a taxi. The sun was directly above. It was excruciatingly hot and damp. I wanted a cheap hotel, but didn't know where to go. Bill tried to persuade me to walk into town. He re-iterated that it was pointless waiting for a cab. He left me. He was wearing white shorts, khaki topee and carried his haversack on his back, a paper bag in one hand and a suit case in the other. I watched him melt into a sea of heat haze. I was irritated that if I got a taxi I would have to foot the whole amount myself. I too was wearing shorts, but I had no hat. I wiped the perspiration from my forehead.

I waited. And waited. Just as I was beginning to think that Bill was right a man turned up and pointed to, what looked like a broken down car across the road, which I thought had been abandoned. He said it was a taxi, did I want it? I said "yes" and when I got into it nearly fell through the floor. Well, what was left of it, for the rutted dusty road was completely visible beneath. My luggage was precariously balanced in the trunk and, after several abortive attempts to crank the engine we were off. We passed Bill and I stopped to offer him a lift. I thought he would jump at the offer.

He replied: "Walking is good for one". And marched off. The last I ever saw of him was that evening in the red light district!

More Stories

The Editor

The trouble with Roland was he was too nice. "Over trusting" is the best nutshell description I can give of him.

I met him in Barbados several years ago. I was bumming around the world and landed pretty well penniless. At the time I was a tall, slender, smooth looking young man. It was precisely because I was so sensitive that I resolved to travel the hard way. I imagined it would toughen me up.

Immediately after my arrival I started looking for a job, I told every employer exactly what I thought he wanted to hear. I lied about my age, experience, academic qualifications. Nobody, however, would give me work. The only person I managed to con (perhaps it was because he too was English) was Roland.

He was editor of the *Barbados Sun*. I remember his blue eyes (spectacled with thick lenses) staring at me, beadlike, as though he wasn't seeing me at all. The dome of his head was huge, resembling a white billiard ball. He was tall, slow moving, diffident. Everything about him was heavy. He looked like an absent-minded professor.

Very soon, however, I discovered he was friendly, easy going, generous. If he realized I knew nothing at all about newspaper work he never commented. On the contrary he went out of his way to be helpful. He wanted me to stay in the efficiency appended to his house at a ridiculously cheap rate. (I didn't because I like my independence and thought it more convenient to live in town.) Nevertheless I was grateful to him for introducing me to people, inviting me to meals, allowing me to drop round more or less when I pleased.

He had just married Clara, a stunning fair-haired English girl, young enough to be his daughter. In London she had been a model. I liked her a lot and we got to know each other well, though not that well as I didn't believe (still don't for that matter) in messing around with other men's wives.

Clara was a terrible flirt. She would kiss me on the lips, play footsy, parade around the house and garden in the thinnest of negligés. It was embarrassing. I think she enjoyed my discomfort, for she often giggled and poked fun at me. Roland said nothing. He peered at us shortsightedly and I got the impression that if we had been making love in the middle of the floor he wouldn't have noticed.

I stayed in Barbados three months and returned just over three weeks ago. Naturally one of the first things I did was to get in touch with Roland. He looked much the same. Maybe a little balder, heavier, more ponderous, but nothing startling. The only major change in his life was Hazel. Clara had left him and he had remarried, he told me the story himself:-

"Shortly after you left a New Zealander, a young aspiring writer like yourself, also going round the world, appeared on the scene. He was broke and needed a job. We were rather overstaffed at the Sun, but I arranged for him to write a column. The pay wasn't good and I helped him out by putting him up cheap in the efficiency and letting him have most of his meals with us. Two months later I learnt that while I was at the office he was carrying on with Clara. The two of them went to New Zealand where, for a while, they lived in sin. I was reluctant to grant a divorce. In a way I vaguely hoped for a reconciliation. But then Hazel turned up and that changed everything."

He told me this the first time I saw him on my return. He spoke calmly, slowly, as though the matter didn't concern him. We were having a drink at his place. Hazel wasn't quite ready. When she came down I was stunned. She was, rather more than a quarter caste. Though attractive, slender, with Caucasian features her color was unmistakable. Like her predecessor Roland was old enough to be her father. She gave me a thin smile and a flabby hand-shake.

No sooner had we exchanged how-do-you-dos than Paul appeared. Tall, slim, clean-cut he looked very fragile. His hair was greased back; he smelt of Eau de Cologne; his nails were manicured. I recognized his South African accent immediately. A photographer, he was living in the efficiency and, like me and this New Zealander, had been taken on by Roland to work for the paper.

The evening was only too familiar. I was thrown back to the performance of a few years earlier. Paul was me. Hazel was Clara. Roland was still Roland. He looked on, said nothing, footsy, giggles, innuendoes. The script was almost identical. Though, in all fairness to myself I was never as blatant as Paul. He and Hazel flirted disgracefully.

Within the next few days I had met some of our mutual friends of old. It was common knowledge that Paul and Hazel were lovers. The only person who didn't know was Roland. When I suggested he be told, all I got was a shrug. The replies were much the same: "It's none of our business"; "we don't want to get involved"; "it's happened once, it'll happen again"; "why hurt the poor guy's feelings"; "he's old enough to look after himself".

One smart ass dismissed the whole thing as a joke: "He should take his specs off, he might see better". The less sympathetic said he deserved what he got. This sort of indifference and in some cases callousness infuriated me. I liked Roland. He had been good to me. I had seen how he had helped others. I resolved to do my damndest for him. I'd show him what friendship meant.

But what to do? If I approached him directly I might do more harm than good. Then, the others had a point: what business was it of mine? I brooded over the matter a good deal. Eventually I came up with what I thought could be a solution. I confront Paul---tell him he was being unfair, even foolish, for he was biting the hand that fed him. There were plenty of other fish in the sea.

A day or two later I lunched with him. Discreetly I got around to the subject that preoccupied me. He was disconcertingly frank. No, he wasn't in love with Hazel. Nor was she with him. They were just having a little fun. Then he laughed: "If her old man can't satisfy her I'm rendering them both a service." He went on when he saw my perplexed expression: "If I quit she quits, and that would make neither of them happy. She likes the comforts he can give her. He's fond of her --- well damn it all he married her."

"That's a load of crap," I protested,

He shrugged. "I don't care what you think. Besides, it's none of your business."

"Roland is my friend. You're making an ass of him."

"Stuff it".

"If I can't appeal to your sense of decency maybe I can appeal to your self-interest. If Roland got to know, you'd lose your job, your cheap accommodation, your almost free board. And if he really wanted to push things to the hilt he probably could get you deported. I can just see Hazel following you to South Africa."

"What are you suggesting?" he snapped.

"That you get out of the apartment. Quit seeing Hazel."

"You've got to be joking."'

"I'm quite serious."

"I think you are," he replied thoughtfully, looking at me intently. "But I can't make you out. I really can't. What do you stand to gain from this?" He stopped, his eyes sparkled: "Unless... unless you fancy the girl yourself."

For a moment I was stunned. Then I spluttered: "You bloody creep. Just because you're a bastard doesn't mean I am. I'd like to break your neck."'

He guffawed.

"You laugh. You may not have many more occasions."'

"What do you propose to do?" he grinned. "Don't tell me I've got to buy myself a water pistol in case you attack me? Or will you get some black ape to do your dirty work for you?"'

"You're a fool," I hissed. "You're quite irresponsible. You wouldn't want Roland to know what you were up to would you?"'

"Hell, I couldn't care less."

I contained my surprise. He spoke as though he meant it.

"Roland won't fire me if that's what you're thinking.'"

"I damn well think he would. He'd have no alternative. If he didn't he'd be the laughing stock of Bridgetown."

"I suppose you're going to put an ad in the paper: `EDITOR CUCKOLDED. WIFE HAS AFFAIR WITH LODGER.'" He grinned. "You know something, I have a shrewd suspicion you may have difficulty getting an announcement like that printed."

"Can't you be serious Paul? I'm trying to help you. You told me yourself that Hazel doesn't mean very much to you. Why can't you leave her alone?"

"Why can't you mind your own business?"

"I've told you, I like Roland.'"

"Well get off my back then."

"Only when you stop chasing his wife."

"I've already told you I'm rendering him a service.'"

"Balls."

"And balls to you," he said rising from the table. "I can see what you're after. It's as plain as pie. The jealousy is oozing out of your ears. You reek of it like a dung heap."

He moved away and I hurried after him. "Wait," I cried. He ignored me, however, and by the time I paid the bill he had vanished.

For the next half hour I walked aimlessly about. I was livid. I hated the bugger. I had expected him to be repentant and cooperative, maybe even frightened. I imagined he would grovel and beg. He looked like a spineless worm. I thought he would act like one. Instead somehow or other, he had got the better of me. And to make out I was jealous was the last straw. God damn it, Hazel wasn't my type at all.

I was so angry I started scheming. I was determined to get my own back, do something really nasty. What? Then it struck me he might have been bluffing at lunch. Perhaps he thought the bold front was the best approach? Maybe spilling the beans to Roland would get him after all?

But Paul was my target, not Roland, I reasoned to myself. How could I hurt one without the other? Then I had an inspiration---a flash of wicked genius. I chuckled. In a trice my mood changed. Of course the whole thing would be a practical joke. Paul, however, might just be silly enough to take me seriously. A guy in the street stopped me and asked what I was laughing at.

A couple of days later I rang Paul at the paper, "Listen you bastard," I said coldly. "I've planted some hash in your apartment. It's well hidden so you won't find it. I wouldn't even bother looking for it if I were you. So if you know what's good for you you'll get the hell out of your place by the end of the month. And quit seeing Hazel. I hope I make myself clear."

"You damn fool."

I hung up.

That evening Roland phoned and asked if he could see me immediately. I sensed the urgency in his voice and agreed. Half an hour later he was offering me a drink in his sitting room. To my surprise Paul and Hazel were also there.

"Paul told me about your call this afternoon," he began. "I think you're out of your mind. Do you realize that breaking into an apartment is a criminal offense? Suppose you had been caught with the pot on you? How would you have explained that? Then somebody could have been listening to your conversation with Paul? Further, if the stuff had been found on the premises it would be my responsibility, since the apartment is mine. I think you were quite thoughtless.."

"I was just playing a practical joke." I grinned. "There is no pot. I haven't been anywhere near your place.

Roland sighed, cupped both hands round his head. "I thought as much. But after your luncheon with Paul Tuesday I couldn't afford to take the risk. He said you were hopping mad."'

I gaped, "Do you mean to say you know about that discussion?"

"Of course I do. Paul came straight back here and told me. You put

184

him in one hell of a dither. He was under the impression you wanted to separate us."

"I don't think I quite understand,." I said

"Precisely. That's your trouble. You're meddlesome, without being observant. At least everybody else here, though blind, minds his own business. And don't think I'm the sightless cretin I'm made out to be. I know exactly what's going on. I am not an editor for nothing."

"If you think there's anything between Hazel and Paul that's part of the game. At one time I thought you might be a participant. But like this New Zealand guy you turned out to be straight, though he didn't have your scruples and he and Clara fell for each other, even though she always told me she was frigid and not much interested in men."

"The present arrangement is not much different from the one I had with Clara, except so far," he smiled thinly towards his wife "Hazel has not let me down."

"Well, there it is, I've had to tell you the truth. Nobody in Barbados, outside these four walls, knows it. People here are remarkably intolerant. In my position I couldn't afford a scandal --- not that kind anyway."

I stared at him incredulously. I was flabbergasted.

He continued: "Now comes the most painful part of what I have to tell you. I like you. Don't misunderstand me. It's just that I don't dare take any chances. I had to do the same with the New Zealander. And that's why I wouldn't give Clara her independence immediately. As long as she wanted a divorce I had a hold over her: I knew she wouldn't talk. "When Hazel came along, however, the position changed. We lived together and once again I had an alibi of normality. I then felt it safe to give Clara what she wanted. And now and again, just in case she has any bright ideas, I send her a small present to sugar her life. She always liked comfort.

"The guy, on the other hand, was a different matter. Obviously, he knew about me. The only hold I had over him, if any, was their desire to marry. That, however, wasn't enough. They both wanted to remain in

Barbados and I wanted them off the island, as far away as possible."

His lips quivered into a smile: "This is where the irony of your little joke comes in. You see I had some pot planted in the efficiency and when it was raided he was accused of possession and later deported. He left under a cloud and that is precisely how I wanted it. That Clara subsequently followed him perhaps made me look a little bit of a fool, but it at least branded him, both of them for that matter, as a couple of near-do-wells. It also meant, what with a police record, that he would probably have to go back home. And that my dear fellow is where you'll have to go. At this very moment, while we are quietly sitting here, some hash is being planted in your apartment. Later you will be raided and events will take their course... "

"That's monstrous," I cried jumping to my feet. "You're positively evil."

He smiled. "The idea was yours."

"I was joking.'"

"Well I'm not."

He offered me another drink, but I refused. I wanted to leave his poisonous atmosphere as quickly as possible. It also struck me if I got back to my apartment in time I might find the hash before the police. A few minutes later I was speeding towards Bridgetown. However, when I arrived the Force was already there. The manager had opened the door and was looking on.

I watched as cupboards and drawers were opened and the linings and pockets of my clothes were examined as well as under the carpets, easy chairs, bed, below the toilet lid--- they searched everywhere. They said they had been tipped off about me. But after about an hour they gave up and left. I was shaken. I was so amazed that I started looking for the pot myself. It was while I was going through my things that the phone rang.

"April Fool," said Roland.

"You ... you... "

"Just remember the next time it really could be there. In the mean time I hope you'll keep a secret."

"You bastard," I cried, though I couldn't help laughing.

"I'm not really. Though the New Zealander was deported for possession I had nothing to do with it. As for the divorce we got it exactly at the end of the statutory requirement---three years."

"Well I'll be damned."

"You certainly will be if you don't keep your mouth shut." Then he asked me round for a drink the following evening.

"As long as it's not poisoned,"'I chaffed.

"Take your chances."

A few minutes later I began the grisly task of tidying the apartment.

The Witch

When I'm tense (and tonight I've got good reason to be) I hop into my Mini Minor and go shooting off to one of the casinos. There are two in Freeport, about five miles apart. At this time everywhere else is pretty well dead. I need the bright lights, the hustle and bustle, the jingle of slot machines to alleviate myself from the pressure of worries. Believe me I've plenty of them. It's 1970, not a vintage year in The Bahamas for landlords and I'm a landlord. I'd just separated a couple in one of my apartments, sort of fencing with machetes! Frankly, I don't know how I had the guts. I'm only five foot six. No athlete. Not even that young: I'm 42, though I suppose I could pass for less. My figure is slender. (I watch it.) Most of my hair is black and I've plenty of it. As for my face it's long, but still youthful I think. Except that I have to wear glasses I'm really quite happy about my looks. My nose is straight, the jaw firm: it's on the whole a very balanced face. I thought of the broken window. That I'd have to pay for, for sure. I toyed with the idea of going for a swim but that's something you do with a woman and tonight I'm on my own. Sunrise Highway twists and turns like a mountain road though the island is as flat as a doormat. Here and there between pines you see specs of light from apartment houses. Some people call Freeport a Cement Jungle. When the money was rolling in I thought it beautiful!

I first came here in 1963. In those days it was no more than a straggling village; but what a village! It was love at first sight! The only thing there, was the dream. Freeport would be another Las Vegas! In twenty years it would have a population of a quarter of a million. There were fortunes to be made and, like so many others, I came to make mine. We wanted to be on the ground floor. We were pioneers. We would shape our world in our own image. Hotels, apartment complexes, shopping centers, roads and marinas began to spring up as though there was a gold rush. Construction went on twenty four hours a day. I would wander around in the car looking at a cocktail of architectural styles: Chinese, Japanese, Spanish, a variety of duplexes. There were even skyscrapers envisaged. Helicopters would land on the tops. Freeport would be a Disneyland to live in!

The money poured in. We thought in millions, though most of us probably only handled a few thousand. I took my life savings out of England and put them in The Bahamas. In the early years the men outnumbered the women four to one. That was good for the professional girls. They came in droves. They came again and again like salmon returning to their breeding grounds. Prostitution was illegal, but in those days (the good old days) the rewards were worth the risks. The whores hovered round the casinos (the first was opened in 1962), for the most part as inconspicuous as the Empire State building. When I was stuck, without a girl, depressed for one reason or another (or none) I would pick myself a 'quickie'. I didn't give a damn about the money. It was coming in like a jackpot win from a slot machine. Even now when things are not going well I don t begrudge myself. I always say a man should cultivate his vices as meticulously as his virtues. I don't smoke, drink, gamble. I suppose the only reason I've never married is that I enjoy sex! That particular night, with my foot hard down on the accelerator, I wondered what I would find. I was determined to forget; if only for a short time.

I swerved and jammed on the brakes. You silly bitch, I yelled at the windscreen. I slowed down and pulled over. I had some choice words ready for her. But as I saw her approach in the mirror my thoughts wandered elsewhere. She was oriental, slender with long black hair. She seemed to be wearing pantaloons, top to match. She walked like an angel. Her head popped in at the window.

"Can you give lide to casino?" she said in English as though it was Chinese.

I told her to hop in.

The pantaloons were black and orange. Her breasts perked out invitingly, though the flesh was well concealed under her peculiar gear. Huge earrings in the shape of pagodas hung from her ears. She was heavily made up, her face white like a mime's, plenty of mascara. I didn't know what the perfume was, but there was plenty of that too.

"You could have got yourself killed," I told her.

"I wanted lide."

"You nearly got yourself one in a hearse."

"What is hearse?"

"Never mind. I'm going to have a snack at the casino. Will you join me?"

She replied she had eaten, but would keep me company with coffee. Five minutes later I was parking. The *El Morocco* Casino, white and yellow on the outside, is a sort of hybrid between a mosque and a fort. It does have a dome and four minarets. For the rest I can imagine the soldiers with their muskets hiding behind the parapets. Inside, the place is bright ---all show and glitter. It is huge. In 1970 I think it was the largest casino in the world. Freeporters were proud of it. I led the way into the coffee shop, small and cozy in comparison with everything else. We found a corner table. I ordered a Hot Roast Beef sandwich and a coffee for Yoko, who sat opposite me against the wall. I told her she was beautiful. She dismissed the remark with a little grunt and a curl of her lips. But I meant what I said. She was stunning. The increased light did her credit. Her features were delicate and harmonious. Her skin was smooth and tight. Decked up as she was she looked a little unreal, as though she was a Japanese doll. The only thing I didn't like about her were her numerous rings. She had about half a dozen on each hand. There was one in particular I thought awful. It was large, black and oval. It looked like the back of a beetle. It gave me the creeps. Her finger nails were very long.

"Tell me about yourself," I said.

She didn't need much encouragement. She told me she had been with the Japanese troupe at *El Morocco*; but now it had disbanded and she was lingering, enjoying the sun. She had no plans and very little money. She was living with two men (platonic, she assured me), but wanted to move out because she found it embarrassing when they brought home their girl friends. She stared at me hardly blinking. Her voice was deep (not exactly feminine) and she had a tendency to confuse her R's and L's, V's and B's. I placed her in the mid thirties. A wild guess of course. A woman's age is inscrutable and that of an oriental one more so. The waiter brought me my sandwich and warned me the plate was very hot. Yoko already had her coffee.

There was a pause. I made a quick decision. "I've got a spare room in my apartment," I said. "You can have it if you want. It's quite independent. It has its own private bathroom. You'll be able to come and go as you please."

"No charge?" she replied, as though expecting the invitation.

"No charge."

"No slings attached?"

I smiled. "No strings attached."

She then said she wanted to see the room.

For a few moments I ate in silence. She watched me. Then asked what I did with myself? I told her about my apartments, that I had four vacancies, another one pending at the end of the month. I was slowly going broke. Perhaps not so slowly?

"You're lucky to hab money to go bloke". Then added: "But look on the blight side. Things never bad as seem. You see I been lucky. I met you and now I got loom to go. What sign are you?"

"Capricorn."

"Me Capricorn too."

"Capricorns get on well with their own sign," I smiled.

She ignored the innuendo, or failed to appreciate it. Instead she told me how a gypsy in San Francisco had accurately predicted her future. She was booked in a Cairo night club. It was definite. Already she had her air ticket. The gypsy said she wouldn't go. She would go to New Orleans and meet a tall dark handsome man whose first initial would begin with S. She beamed, rubbed her hands as though with pleasure.

The Six Day war changed everything. In New Orleans she met the man, but things did not work out.

I pushed my plate aside and took her hands in mine. I felt the texture of the skin, the flexibility of the fingers. After a little more study I gave her a brief character analysis. Then I told her she would very shortly be having an affair. She would stay in Freeport longer than expected and with me longer than she intended.

She laughed, pulling her hands away. "I don't know I stay with you yet." She stood up. "But let go see apartment."

Half an hour later the decision was made. She liked the apartment. She liked the room, which was large and carpeted, with plenty of closet space and a huge double bed. There was a private bathroom as I had promised. The kitchen, which she examined carefully, also met with her approval. "I come tomorrow," she said. Then informed me, without a flicker of a smile, that she was a witch and because I had done her a favor she would do me one: she would use her powers to fill my apartments.

"Thanks," I grinned. "That's exactly what I need. If while you're about it you can arrange for a rent increase too, that'll be more than welcome."

She stamped her foot. Her eyes blazed. "You think I not serious. I bely serious. You see... I hab bely, strong powers. How do you think I get lide to casino, new loom for myself?"

I didn't answer.

"I can't fill your apartments by myself," she continued, "you must help."

"What do I have to do?"

"I explain later."

She then covered her face with her hands, her fingers spread, as though she was an infant playing peekaboo. The back of the beetle stared at me.

"What are you doing?" I said,

No reply. I thought she might be praying. The thought of appealing to the Almighty to fill my units hadn't occurred to me. I watched her fascinated. Was she some kind of nut, I wondered?

She opened one eye and stared between two fingers. "No obligations on my part?"

I reassured her.

"Good." She brought her hands down and with her right one took mine. "We have business deal. You give me loom. No funny stuff. I fill apartments."

Bewildered, I shook hands.

The following evening she explained my contribution to filling my units. We were in the kitchen. I was hovering behind her. She was making herself a bean shoot, zucchini, mushroom soup. (She was, she said, a vegetarian).The effort I had to make was entirely mental: I had to visualize full occupancy. All it required was the right attitude of mind.

"How can I see my apartments full when they aren't ?"

"You must not think like that. That negative thinking. You think positively."

"It makes no difference," I replied. "I've got vacancies because of deteriorating political, economical conditions. When they get better, which I don't see happening in the immediate future, my situation will improve."

She gave an unladylike snort. She stirred the soup. She repeated I had to think positively. I had to concentrate. She couldn't do everything on her own. I was blocking all the good she was doing.

"I don't exactly see what good you are doing?" I said perhaps somewhat tactlessly." Then, as though adding injury to insult, continued : "This morning another of my tenants gave me notice."

She turned on me, her nostrils flaring, waving the wooden spoon. "How can I fill apartments," she cried angrily, "when you don't want them full? You send out only negative lays. And one negative lay is more powerful than ten positive ones."

"You mean rays." My eyes twinkled.

"LAYS," she shouted.

"How about coming out to dinner with me?" I said. "I want to be amused. And you can amuse me. You can put the soup in the refrigerator. It'll keep."

She beamed. "You see my powers. I had nothing to do this evening and I wanted to be invited out Now you've invited me to dinner. That's positive thinking!"

I swallowed. "You really are a witch," I said

She took this as a compliment. She gave me a Chicago hug, that is to say our bodies didn't touch. "You see, bery soon apartments fill up."

In the car she told me how she had made $2,000. She had been short of cash and needed some in a hurry. She wanted $2,000: no more, no less. She concentrated very hard. Nothing would stop her getting it. She was convinced, completely sure, positive. She went to the casino and an hour later emerged with exactly two grand.

"Why did you stop at two thousand?" Again I asked tactlessly. "If it had been me I would have aimed for two million!"

"I only needed $2,000."

We went to the Italian restaurant candle-lit with red tablecloths and in the background soft music and a slight aroma of pasta. She had ratatouille and rice, apple juice. I had piccata, white wine. Instead of amusing me she gave me a lecture: Norman Vincent Peale. Hubbard, Rampa, Napoleon Hill, Dale Carnegie and others I was not familiar with. Once I tried to take her hand, but she pulled it away. She reminded me of my promise and warned me if I tried any funny stuff she would stop helping me with my apartments. She extolled the virtues of yoga, meditation, positive thinking. She informed me that she was a fifth initiate, whatever that might mean. Apparently I was a third. I listened in spite of myself. If my attention strayed she sensed it. I wondered if the reward was worth the price. Press on regardless. I suggested we take in a show and go dancing.

"Me fix to meet somebody. Maybe late show."

"Not for me. I have to be up early in the morning. Another time."

She took my hand. "You not angly?"

"No."

I paid the check. She wanted to be dropped off at the casino, so I took her there. In the car she elaborated on positive thinking. I kept quiet. I had no doubt that thoughts could influence. I didn't think I could fill my units that way, though it did strike me that if I saw Yoko more positively she might be more responsive towards me.

I eyed myself critically in the mirror. I was clean shaven. I had been to the hair dresser that morning. I smelt mildly of deodorant and after shave lotion. I was wearing grey flannels, brown leather jacket; underneath a green waist coat and white shirt. The tie was bright orange and my shoes were black and glistened as though they were varnished. I looked good I thought. The occasion was my birthday and the first outing with Yoko since we had dined at the Italian restaurant. Over six weeks had elapsed since then. Incredible as it may seem, though we lived in the same apartment, I hardly ever saw her. She was a night owl. I was a day one. Sometimes our paths crossed during the early part of the evening, when she was rising and I getting ready to go out for dinner. The first thing she would do is prepare her soup. She wore sandals and a Kimono-like dressing gown. Unmade-up her face was pasty. Her eyes always had a tired look about them. We would chat a while.

"You know the two tenants who were going to leave at the end of the month. Well, they're staying."

Then a few days later I told her about another unit being filled.

She extolled the virtues of positive thinking and her powers as a witch.

"Yes, I must admit, since you've been around things are looking better."

On the rare occasions that we saw each other I did learn a little more about her. I gathered she went to a few parties, hung around bars and men. She hadn't much good to say for the men. According to her they were all creeps, "Creep" was one of her favorite words. She didn't want to get married. She had seen what had happened to her mother: At her husband's beck and call twenty four hours a day--- cook, cleaning woman, nurse-maid, rubber inflated doll --- a slave, there was no other way of describing her . Yoko escaped when she was 14. Arriving in the States was like a breath of fresh air. She approved of Women's Lib, though wasn't a Libber. She had taken to dancing like a cat takes to climbing trees. She had been all over the world. One day, when she got too old for dancing, she would go into interior decorating; open her own establishment. In the mean time she was enjoying herself.

"Don't you like men?"

"They're all creeps, I sock-it to them."

"What about love?"

She shrugged.

These are the sort of tidbits I picked up from her the few times we were together. On some occasions she would sleep out altogether. Now and again I would meet her in the morning just as I was going out and she was returning, bleary eyed, from her night's prowl. I had invited her out to dinner, dancing, shows, the movies, even a trip to Miami. There was always an excuse. The first few times I took them at face value. Then I began to get irritated. I felt she was using me. She would sense my mood and remind me of our agreement. She was filling her end of the bargain. She had nothing against me personally. It was absolutely true she was booked up. The only reason she had agreed to go out with me tonight was because it was my birthday. The outing had been arranged three weeks earlier. It was like making an appointment with the President of General Motors. As a present she had given me a fat wooden Buddha for good luck. She had left it on the coffee table in the lounge neatly wrapped in red paper with a blue ribbon. On the Birthday card she had added "POSITIVE THINKING from YOKO".

I was waiting in the sitting room, L-shaped, with the dining space on the side adjoining the kitchen. I was flipping through the Freeport Gazette. Yoko was never on time. The men who collected her always rang to check if she was ready. They came and went as anonymously as visitors at a museum. Most of those I saw were middle-aged with a smart sugar-daddy look about them. Yoko claimed she gave them nothing. As she was always near broke that was perhaps true. Where her money came from I don't know, though she did tell me now and again when she won at the tables. That she could keep herself this way I have my doubts. Still, with her anything is possible.

Then there was the time I thought I might gain some sort of hold on her. I was piqued by her inaccessibility, as though she was a goddess or something. Anyway, I surmised (quite rightly as things turned out) that her immigration papers would not be in order. After all she had come into the Colony with the troupe, no doubt on a special visa. I couldn't imagine her adjusting her status without being pushed to it. Sure enough she had done nothing. That was when I suggested she hop-over to Miami and return as a tourist, all quite legal. The following evening she showed me her passport. Somehow, she never told me how (except to remind me she was a witch) she had got an extension for two months. I suppose the only positive thing I can say about all this is that I wasn't being duped like all the other dopes who were taking her out; she wasn't giving me that privilege.

Tonight, of course, would be different. It was my birthday. I had already bought her her birthday present (due in a few days) a turquoise ring from the local Tiffany. (I'd seen her admiring it there). Maybe I would give it to her to climax the evening? We were to dine and see the new show at the casino. *El Morocco* is tops. I waited. She was already half an hour late, but she kept yelling through the door that she would be out in a moment. Eventually she did appear. She stood in the passage so that I could admire her. She flung her arms above her head, stuck a leg out, froze her grin, all like a chorus girl. Actually she looked more Chinese than Japanese. She wore an all black dress, slits down the sides, a high neck piece elaborately embroidered with lace, a long sparkling necklace. All in good taste. Her hair was piled high, but her silver shoes had low heels. (I suppose out of consideration for my five foot six). I went and gave her a hug. She responded.

"Thanks for the present," I said. "It's already brought me luck. This morning I got two more tenants. That's a record. One is moving in immediately. The other on the 15th."

"You see what I do," she beamed.

"You're wonderful. But we must go."

It was shortly after 2:30 in the morning when the show ended. The dinner had been fine and the show excellent. We lingered as the crowds filed out.

"Bery nice ebening," said Yoko.

"You know what I want now."

She stared at me.

I was going to say her body, but other words came out: "I would like to go swimming."

"Water bely cold."

"Be a sport." She hesitated. Then said we would have to go back to the apartment so she could get her swim suit.

"We can swim in the nude."

Her face froze. She shook her head.

"There's no harm," I said. "You go on stage without a stitch. A swim in the raw is healthy. And besides, I'll let you into a little secret: it won't be the first time I've seen a naked woman."

"I not nudie. All other girls in show nudies. I dance."

"I think you're being ridiculous."

She stood up, her eyes were blazing. "I not funny stuff girl. I tell you truth when I meet you. Yoko not hide anything." She stormed away.

I followed her from the show room and through the casino. She went to the Ladies and I hung around waiting for her. Then, after a few minutes, still feeling irritated, I began to wander. I like roaming along the tables, between the rows of one arm bandits. I'm not interested in the gambling, but I do eye the women. Here and there I stop ostensibly to watch a game, covertly to ogle. The waitresses, wearing cocktail smiles and low cut dresses, scurry to and fro. I can't see a single whore. A pretty woman drifts by leaving a trail of perfume behind her. She has an escort. It strikes me the heat is too high, or the profits too low. Clearly the oldest profession has wiped Freeport off the map. I console myself: nobody ever died of sex starvation. I resolve to call it a night. No point in aggravating myself further.

Soon I was in bed. I tried to read. When I couldn't concentrate I switched the lights off. But I couldn't sleep. I wondered if I'd be able to get a refund for the turquoise. Yoko was a bitch. It struck me scores of girls would have thrown themselves at me for a free room. I could think of none. I contemplated an ad in the Gazette. While I was mentally formulating the precise words I would use, the phone rang. It was past 3:30 a.m.. I imagined it would be the witch/bitch. I was inclined not to answer, but did all the same. A woman's voice, high pitched, barely comprehensible, said something about Yoko. I replied she was out. Then she made me understand it was me she wanted to see: it was very important. She had to come at once. Would I pay for the cab, she wanted to know? I asked if there had been an accident. No, she said, but still insisted she come immediately. I yielded.

Half an hour later my bell rang. I opened the door in my dressing gown. I had my wallet in my hand. She grabbed some money for the driver. The glimpse I had had of her told me she was Japanese, young and slender, a bit too skinny for my taste. She wore a thin black dress, almost a negligé, for her breasts were struggling to spill over the top. When she returned she smiled sweetly and introduced herself as Mitsuko. Her face was pale and frightened. Naturally the eyes were brown, the hair black, elaborately piled high with combs, like a geisha's.

It could have been a wig. I invited her to be seated and suggested a drink. She sat down, but refused the drink.

"What can I do for you?" I asked.

Her English was appalling; but eventually I understood she needed money. She wasn't a prostitute, she assured me. All she wanted was $50 and she would sleep with me.

"Who sent you?"

She didn't understand, or pretended not to. However, when I told her I hadn't $50 she understood me well enough. (Earlier that evening I'd used my Amex card.) I offered her a check. Instead of replying she went into my bedroom. When she realized it wasn't what she wanted she went into the other room, Yoko's. She hiked up the mattress, found a slit in it, pulled out a handkerchief and unfolding it revealed a wad of notes. She counted $50, then put everything back exactly as it was. She explained, in her garbled way, that I could replace the money after going to the bank in the morning.

"Does Yoko make her money like you?" I asked.

"Yoko make plenty money."

I felt a renewed surge of anger. So that's what she was. I might have guessed. I should have offered her cash in the first place. Why hadn't she asked? Surely not pride? Women are a riddle. Yoko was a riddle wrapped in mystery.

Though I would have gladly watched Yoko on the rack I did have a prick of conscience about using her money. Mitsuko had already put it in her bag. She went into the bedroom. I hesitated, then followed her. Mitsuko, just before leaving, again assured me she wasn't a prostitute. I felt much better, a little high. I hopped into bed as though I was a ten year old. Buried, between the sheets, hugging a pillow, I knew how I would tackle Yoko.

I sat up abruptly. A wave of fear shot through me. I don't know whether I heard a scream or dreamt it. My first thought was that the building was on fire. An instant later my door was flung open, the light switched on. Yoko was there, still in her evening clothes, feet astride, lips trembling, cheeks twitching, eyes almost popping out of their sockets. I thought she was having a stroke. At first I couldn't make out what she was saying.

"What's happened?" I said feebly, clutching the sheets.

"You steal my money," she shrieked. "You thief. You no good man creep. You see, I sock-it to you. I empty all apartments. I punish you good, hard. No one make fool of Yoko". She stopped abruptly and left the room.

I crouched clasping my knees, half sitting, half lying. A thousand thoughts were shooting through my head. I could tell the truth. I could deny everything, just give her the $50 and done with it. Or I could say my maintenance man had repaired the bed. The cleaning woman had been in. Maybe a thief had come in. I felt hot and cold. She could check with the maintenance man, the cleaning woman. I jumped out of bed. Perhaps she had planned the whole thing with Mitsuko? I went into her bedroom without knocking. She was sitting on the bed, leaning forward, holding her head in her hands. She looked up.

"I want you to know that I haven't touched your money. There's no reason why I should. On the other hand if there's been a theft on my premises I feel partly responsible. I'll make good your loss"

"You pay me $550." Her tone sounded more like a command than a statement..

I felt myself sway. I must have looked as though I had been hit across the head. I pulled the chair from the dresser and sat down.

"You were robbed of $550?" I repeated eventually, still gaping, my voice subdued. "It's not possible".

She flared: "Me not lie."

After a pause I told her to start at the beginning. She told me where she kept her money and it had gone. It struck me she might be lying. Alternatively Mitsuko could have slipped back into her room without my noticing. I told her about her friend.

"I see Mitsuko an hour ago and she tell me nothing."

I gave a forced laugh. "Of course not. Why should she?"

"She not know where I hide money."

"I think you planned this together."

She jumped up and stamped her foot. "Not twue."

"How is it you had so much money? You're always telling me you're broke."

"Yesterday I won at casino."

"I might have guessed."

"You give me money back."

"Yes. I'll return the $50. And that's it. And you'd better start looking for somewhere else to stay. I won't keep you any more."

Her eyes flashed. She raised her hands, her finger bent so that her long nails pointed at me. They looked like claws. I thought she was going to pounce, maybe scratch me. I covered my face. But she didn't move and looked straight through me, muttering something under her breath. I presume a curse. I left the room.

It was shortly after 9:30 that my manager/maintenance man got me on the phone. He told me that one of the tenants had quit in the middle of the night. Somebody else, he didn't know who, had emptied some glue over the washing machines coin slots in the utility room. He said he was trying to get it off with boiling water; but he thought the mechanism for the quarters was irretrievably damaged and would have to be replaced. I told him I'd come at once. I hung up and went into the bathroom. I was feeling angry and helpless. I sluiced my face, head and the back of my neck with cold water. I took a couple of Anacin. I shaved and showered; and while drying myself was once more interrupted by the phone. Again my maintenance man. More good news! The main drain was blocked: several of the apartments were beginning to smell. In one of them muck was backing up. The snake was needed. He couldn't get hold of a plumber. I said I'd see what I could do. Then, for the next hour I was on the phone. Eventually the most expensive plumbers in town agreed to come within the hour.

The nightmare continued all day. When, after my luncheon snack, I went to check the washing machines the plumber still hadn't arrived. Half the building reeked of stale urine. The apartment where the back-up had started stank like an open cess pit. The tenants said they would quit. I tried to placate them by putting deodorant sticks in every room and liberally sprinkling the soggy carpets with perfume. I spent the whole afternoon hanging around: calling the plumbers again and again. I scrubbed the coin mechanisms in the laundry room. I listened to complaints. As best I could I pacified the tenants, even to the extent of playing with their dogs and children. Fortunately by evening the toilets were working, though the stink lingered and was liable to do so for days. When I got back home Yoko had already cleared out.

The list of my requirements was hardly the kind you take to the local Safeway, or any other supermarket for that matter. Apparently, to name just a few of the things I had to get included dried bits of wild cat, powder from a dead man's bones, human dung, a puppy's intestines, half a pint of my blood, some herbs and one live hen! I dug up this information, with considerable trouble from (so I was told) a Voodoo priest. I had several Haitians living in my Down Town units (where I was staying) who, with persuasion and bribery, all shrouded in secrecy, took me to see one sinister looking man after another. Once the paraphernalia had been collected I was to return for the exorcism. In the mean time I had to walk around with a slab of liver in each shoe at all times. That, and a substantial fee, (I was informed) was the price I'd have to pay to cleanse myself of Yoko!

I am a sensible man, a rational man, a Westerner. I believe in the Father, the Son and the Holy Ghost. I have dabbled in astrology, palmistry and sometimes played with an Ouija board, but these are only parlor games. I don't take them seriously. I maybe a little superstitions, but I've never believed in black magic, witchcraft or any of that other hocus pocus. (When Yoko was staying with me I was humoring her. That's a fact. God's truth.) Now. Well, I don't know what to think. I'm a bundle of nerves. I'm not sleeping well. My appetite is poor. I've lost weight. My face is pasty, my eyes permanently red. All this in ten days. Then, as though the evidence of my health and appearance weren't enough I have six vacancies. One would think the plague had struck my apartment buildings. But I haven't just lost tenants. I've lost them with headaches: smashed furniture, some stolen, kids crayoning the walls, a child bitten by a dog, a police raid for marijuana, a break-in and a rape.

Really, it's amazing I haven't had a nervous breakdown. Of course I've thought of throwing myself at Yoko's mercy. But then I find it hard to believe she's responsible for all this. After all (as I've just said) I'm a twentieth century man. Spells just don't happen. I'm having a run of bad luck, that's all. The trouble is things are getting worse; by the day---by the hour. I consulted the Voodoo priest out of curiosity. Well, perhaps not entirely. My pride is at stake. The thought of crawling back to Yoko, my tail between my legs, groveling and licking her feet is not a picture I like entertaining. Then there is always the possibility she might ignore me, curl her lips and walk away. On the other hand the Voodoo holy man might do no more than take my money, waste my time, demonstrate what an ass I am. I can just see myself drilling some bones, drying a cat out on the clothes line, displaying an array of stool samples, like at the laboratory of some hospital. Oh, and I was nearly forgetting --- the squelchy cool raw liver, with all the cats and dogs in Freeport at my feet. Ha. Ha. This is so funny I could cry.

What to do? So far all I've done is procrastinate and procrastination is the thief of time; and, as everybody knows time is money. And money, as Somerset Maugham has pointed out, is a kind of sixth sense, for you can't use the other five without it. The next thing I did, with the turquoise in my pocket, was to go where I had bought it. In the frenzy of the last ten days I had forgotten it. The shop was in the International Bazaar.

In and Around the Caribbean

The windows were full of glitter like a score of candelabra. A heavy black guard dressed like a general on ceremonial parade, hovered around the door. Inside the atmosphere was plush and grand, air-conditioned and scented. There were about half a dozen display tables. At one of them stood Yoko, gesticulating, speaking her English/Chinese. I was about to slip away, when the lady help, suddenly looking up, pointed at me as though I was a wanted criminal. "Sir," she cried, and scurried over to me like a flustered bird.

"Aren't you the gentleman who bought a turquoise ring here about two weeks ago?"

I took a small box out of my pocket, opened it and spread the thin protective tissue. "Is this it?" I said.

Yoko grabbed it. "This the one .... I buy...."

"Madam, it belongs to..."

"I pay more....". She stopped and looked at me fixedly.

I answered her stare. Then, after a pause cooly informed her it wasn't for sale.

"Come. We go talk." She put her arm through mine, but I held steady.

"The ring please."

She gave it back to me. I let myself be guided towards the door.

"Madam, sir....". The lady help (I think the owner) flurried after us, her arms flapping. "If there is any transaction you should come back to me."

We went to the coffee shop in the casino. With the ace of trumps in my pocket I was feeling much better than I had for a long time.

As soon as we sat down she congratulated herself on her powers. She had willed whoever had the gem to come into the store at that moment. Then she asked what I wanted for it? Or was it for one of my numerous girl friends?

"It was for you. It was going to be your birthday present."

Her jaw dropped. "You get turquoise ling for me?" she said

incredulously.

I nodded. Then added, smiling faintly: "Nor did I steal your money in order to buy it."

She covered her face with her hands. She spread two fingers. An eye opened and stared at me through two beads: a brown one next to a black beetle.

"Maybe Mitsuko take money?" she said eventually.

"I think so."

"You give me ling now?" she pressed, lowering her hands, grinning, her tone pleading.

"A lot has happened since you left me. You did a very wicked thing to me."

Silence. Her wide eyes held steady.

"If I give you the turquoise will you take your spell off me?"

She laughed. "But you no believe in my powers!"

"Perhaps not. But all I know is an awful (I mean awful) lot has happened to me since you cleared out. I want you to come back and stay with me."

She cocked her head to one side. "Not possible now. Me have to go to Puerto Rico in ten days for new show."

"How do I get rid of the curse you put on me?"

She frowned, sucked in her lips. "Vely difficult .... Me send out bely strong negative lays." She shook her head two or three times; then stopped and began nodding: "There bely strong antidote. Bely strong. Me never use. But I think maybe work."

"Just tell me what it is."

Then she told me: I would have to get dried bits of wild cat, powder from a dead man's bones, human dung, a puppy's intestines, a live hen. Also half a pint of my blood. She'd get the herbs.......

I cut her short. "Will you come to the Supermarket with me? We can get the liver immediately"

Reading Palms

Ha. Ha. That's good, good," cried the Swami jocularly. "You would do very well in my country. They would make you a Holy man, a saint. You would have no need of my services ". I was so engrossed in the hand reading that I didn't realize a small group had gathered around me The Swami dismissed me with a flick of his hand: "Thank you. Thank you very much ... Very good, good." Then he spoke a little more seriously. "But you must not take these things seriously. It is only a game, a little fun. The future is in God's hands. Only He, and He alone, knows it ... But very good George, good."

We were in the small alcove, stone floored, with pictures of Indian Holy men on the walls, a smell of incense pervaded the air. The Swami returned to his position facing us and crossed his legs in the lotus position. I returned to my space on the floor and sat on my heels.. It was customary to have a final few minutes silence before the evening broke up. I closed my eyes and started to count my breaths.

Outside you could hear the swishing of the sea, the eternal ebbing and flowing as Swamiji[1] would say, a sound that had gone on for billions of years and would continue for billions more.

"Listen to the silence," said the Swami. "Deep, deep down inside you will find peace ---the peace that passes all understanding."

Then there was quiet, absolute silence.

There was no peace for me however. I could not concentrate. My mind was buzzing with a thousand thoughts, disjointed, helter-skelter, a sort of panic feeling. I liked the girl sitting next to me. What had brought me to the camp? The wind whistled gently. Were the others really meditating? Why couldn't I? I liked this sun drenched strip of coast, with palms almost up to the sea; the water a light blue you found nowhere else. Everything is so beautiful. Concentration camps. Ugh. It

---

[1] An affectionate name for Swami

was still quite light outside and the moon was full and peaceful. I could see it glistening silver on the sea. I thought of the swim we would have a little later. But Christ I was restless. God give me peace, peace. Anyway, I had been a success at the social part of the evening. Now, I'm beginning to get pins and needles in my feet. Why do these moments of silence seem like hours? I can't keep still any longer . Oh God.

"OM...OM.."[2]

I joined in with the chorus of voices.

A few minutes later the evening broke up. Immediately I found myself surrounded by an excited little group. A score of hands were thrust in front of me. "Will you read my palm." "How do you do it?" "Me ... Me.." "Where did you learn?" "You're very good. You said something you couldn't possibly have known." "Please read my hand. It's very important. I must know something."

I yielded. I took a pair of hands in mine, examined them, squeezed them, tested them for flexibility. Then I began speaking, speaking as though in a trance. The words just flow out of me. I don't know how I do it. I know what I'm saying, yet I don't. I talk of destiny, love, money, luck, good and bad health, spiritual development, problems, difficulties to overcome. I am quite sincere. I am speaking, but the words are not mine

Of course I couldn't give just one reading. Once I had started I had to go on. Everybody was lapping up every word I said. I was the center of attention. I felt that much of the time I was hitting the mark or anyway pretty close. I don't know how many hands I read. Even the Swami stood around listening, but frankly I didn't like his presence, for he kept interjecting cryptic, humourous, if not critical remarks. "Now you read my hands," he said laughingly and thrust them under my nose.

His hands were thick and pudgy. The head line was long and swooped low towards the mound of Luna. The life line was short, but

---

[2] The sacred symbol of Indian philosophy on which to meditate: a sort of parallel to Amen.

vigorous and strong. It was a hand with passion and energy, as well as imagination. The mound of Saturn was well developed. I waited for the flow of words.

"Tell me if I am going to be a millionaire, like everybody already thinks I am." He chaffed. "The millionaire Swami. You do not know how many people think I am rich. Go on, tell me."

"No, no Swami, I know you too well," I protested.

"I can tell you I have no money," he grinned. "But you tell me about tomorrow. Is anybody going to leave me a million dollars?"

"I don't think so," I replied softly. And I pushed his hands away.

"Won't you read my hands?"

"No, no. That's enough for one night. I've read too many already. I'm tired."

He laughed: "You see it is nonsense. He knows he cannot read my hands because I do not believe. Nobody can make you believe, only God. But good George. Good ... Come let us go for a swim."

I went to my dormitory to put on my trunks. David, who a few moments earlier had been listening to my readings, was already in his when I got to the room.

"Why didn't you want to read Swamiji's hands?" he asked.

"I don't know," I replied. "I just felt I had nothing to say. The words wouldn't come."

That, in fact was the truth. I felt a kind of emptiness, a peculiar sadness I couldn't explain.

"Oh well," he said: "You can't expect to have psychic powers all the time. Even an oracle, I suppose, has to take a rest now and again."

I smiled: 'I don't really believe half the stuff I say. Swamiji is right: it's only a parlor game, a little fun to entertain people."

"I don't quite believe that," David continued: "I think you're being modest. You were uncannily accurate a good deal of the time. I think there's something in it."

I too felt there was vaguely something in it, though I didn't know what. I shrugged: "Come. Lets go."

When we got outside a little crowd was gathered on the beach. We could see something had happened. We joined the others. A man was giving mouth to mouth resuscitation, pumping the lungs furiously to the immobile figure on the ground.

But I knew, even before anybody said anything, there was no hope: Swamiji was already dead.